ALSO by RUTH WHITE

A Month of Sundays
Little Audrey
Way Down Deep
The Search for Belle Prater
Buttermilk Hill
Tadpole
Memories of Summer
Belle Prater's Boy
Weeping Willow
Sweet Creek Holler

The Treasure of Way Down Deep

The Treasure of Way Down Deep

Ruth White

MARGARET FERGUSON BOOKS

FARRAR STRAUS GIROUX
NEW YORK

Farrar Straus Giroux Books for Young Readers
175 Fifth Avenue, New York 10010

Copyright © 2013 by Ruth White
Map copyright © 2007 by Susy Pilgrim Waters for Lilla Rogers Studio
Printed in the United States of America
Designed by Cathy Bobak
First edition, 2013
1 3 5 7 9 10 8 6 4 2

www.mackids.com

Library of Congress Cataloging-in-Publication Data

White, Ruth, 1942–
    The treasure of Way Down Deep / Ruth White. — 1st ed.
        p.   cm.
    Sequel to: Way Down Deep
    Summary: In 1954, when mine closings bring an economic crisis to
Way Down Deep, West Virginia, foundling Ruby Jolene Hurley makes a
thirteenth-birthday wish to find the treasure rumored to have been buried
by one of the town's founders.
    ISBN 978-0-374-38067-0 (hardcover)
    ISBN 978-0-374-37747-2 (ebook)
    [1. Community life—West Virginia—Fiction.   2. Boardinghouses—
Fiction.   3. Buried treasure—Fiction.   4. Dogs—Fiction.
5. Foundlings—Fiction.   6. Orphans—Fiction.   7. West Virginia—
History—1951—Fiction.]   I. Title.

PZ7.W58446Tre 2013
[Fic]—dc22

                                                          2012021665

For Pate

the Treasure of Way Down Deep

WAY DOWN DEEP

ROUND & ROUND

RAILROAD STREET

DEEP CREEK

BUS DEPOT

MORGAN'S DRUGS

BEVINSS BARBER SHOP

THE BEER BARREL

SILVER SCREEN

STATE HIGHWAY 99

← TO YONDER MOUNTAIN

A&P GROCERY STORE

POST OFFICE

LIBRARY

COURTHOUSE

WARD STREET

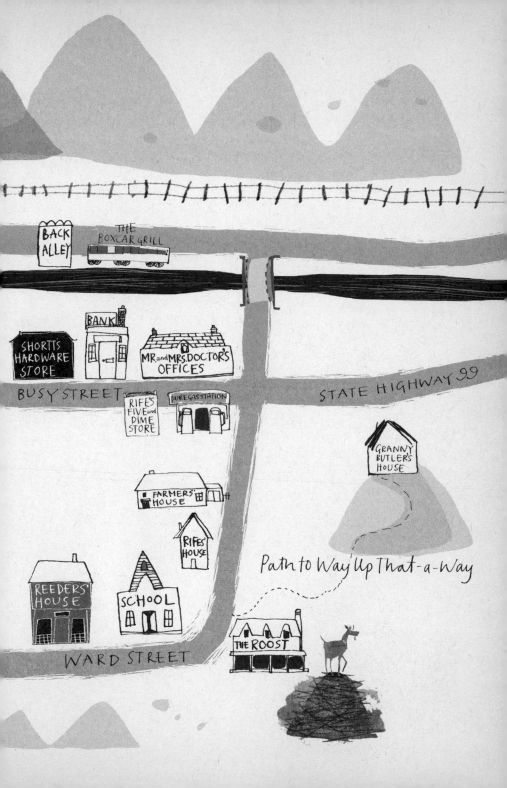

CAST
of
CHARACTERS

ARISTOTLE: a very old and very wise owl

BEAR, MR.: principal of the Way Down Deep school

BEVINS, MR.: the town barber and owner of Bevins's
Barber Shop

BEVINS, MRS.: Mr. Bevins's wife, a volunteer at the school

BEVINS, LANTHA: the Bevinses' teenage daughter

BUTLER, GRANNY: an old albino woman who lives Way Up
That-a-Way

CHAMBERS, MR.: mayor of Way Down Deep and owner of
the A&P Grocery Store

CHAMBERS, SHELBY: bank teller and daughter-in-law of the
mayor

CIRCUIT-RIDING PREACHER

CRAWFORD, A. H.: a boarder at The Roost who is writing a
book about the town

DALES, MR.: president of Way Down Bank

DEEL, ELBERT: a circuit-riding judge

DUKE, MISS: new English teacher from elsewhere

ELKINS, LUCY: a permanent resident at The Roost

EXPERT, MR.: an authority on coins from Washington, D.C.

FARMER, MRS.: the Way Down Deep postmistress

FARMER, MR.: husband to Mrs. Farmer

FULLER, CONNIE LYNN, SUNNY GAYE, AND BONNIE CLARE: the religious Fuller triplets

GENTRY, MR.: the high school band director

GENTRY, MRS.: formerly Miss Worly, the town librarian

GRANDMA: Goldie Combs from Yonder Mountain, Ruby's grandma

HURLEY, RUBY JOLENE: formerly Ruby June, girl who has been raised by Miss Arbutus at The Roost

JETHRO: Ruby's pet goat

JUDE: typesetter apprentice at *The Way Down Deep Daily*

JUSTUS, DR.: the town's physician, called Mr. Doctor

JUSTUS, DR.: the town's dentist, called Mrs. Doctor

LEGHORN, TONY: works at the Shimpock junkyard

MORGAN, MR. AND MRS.: owners of Morgan's Drugs

MORGAN, JUANITA, JUDE, EDNA, AND SLIM: the Morgan children

MULLINS, MR. AND MRS.: owners of the Pure Gas Station and The Boxcar Grill

MULLINS, REESE, MARY NELL, SUSIE, PAULINE, JUNIOR, CLARENCE, AND GERRY JOY: the Mullins children, who help their parents at the gas station and the grill

REEDER, BOB: Robber Bob, formerly a would-be bank robber, and father to five children

REEDER, BIRD: Robber Bob's senile father

REEDER, PETER, CEDAR, JEETER, SKEETER, AND RITA: the
Reeder kids
REYNOLDS, SHERIFF: sheriff of Way Down Deep
RIFE, MRS.: the ninety-year-old owner of Rife's Five and
Dime
RIPPLE: a red fox
SALESMAN OF *THE BOOK OF KNOWLEDGE* ENCYCLOPEDIA
SHORTT, MRS.: owner of Shortt's Hardware Store
SPRINGSTEP, JOHNNY RAY: son of a coal miner who wants to
be a doctor
STACEY, MR.: the milkman
TRIPOD: Ruby's three-legged dog
TRUEHEART, BECKY: a school friend of Ruby's from the
small settlement of Shimpock
WARD, ARCHIBALD: the founder of the town of Way Down
Deep
WARD, MISS ARBUTUS: descendant of Archibald, and
proprietor of The Roost

1

IT WAS SATURDAY, OCTOBER 2, 1954, IN WAY DOWN DEEP, West Virginia, and Ruby Jolene Hurley was celebrating her thirteenth birthday. It was a crisp autumn day, and the sky was a deep blue with a few puffy white clouds floating over the valley. Ruby was in her new room at The Roost, which was the boardinghouse where she had grown up. Only recently had she moved into this room, formerly occupied by Miss Worly, the town librarian. Miss Worly and Mr. Gentry, the high school band director, who had also lived at The Roost, had married and moved into a small house out on Highway 99.

"My spacious pastel boudoir" was how Miss Worly had described this room. She used that term, because, first of all, she liked peppering her sentences with fancy words, and, second, the room was decorated in pink and blue, with a dash of purple here and there, and it was larger than most of the other guest rooms at The Roost. Ruby loved the spacious pastel boudoir.

For a few minutes she lingered in front of the mirror before going downstairs to receive guests for her birthday party. Her new dress was the color of the golden maple leaves outside her window, and her shoes were black patent leather. Ruby's hair, of course, had always been a mass of red ringlets around her face, and her eyes were the color of bluebells. The people of Way Down considered her a natural beauty, but when she looked at her own image in the mirror, she was far more critical. She thought her hair was way too thick and wild, and too curly. And she thought she could have done without some of those freckles.

Downstairs in the common room Ruby found that her guests were arriving and were being greeted by Lucy Elkins and Ruby's Grandma Combs, both permanent residents of the boardinghouse. Miss Arbutus Ward, owner of The Roost, was also there. She was a direct descendant of Archibald Ward, who had first discovered Way Down Deep in the eighteenth century, and the last Ward still living in the town. Miss Arbutus had raised Ruby since she was a toddler and was like a mother to her.

The Reeders had come dressed in their finest, which wasn't to say much, but they were clean, and good-looking, every blessed one of them, starting with Peter, who was the same age as Ruby, and the boy she liked more than any other; Cedar, barely twelve; the identical twins Jeeter and Skeeter, nine; and the only girl, Rita, just turned six. They had moved to Way Down this past June when their stumpy little daddy, Robber Bob, had made a feeble attempt at robbing the bank—thus the nickname. Naturally, the bank president, Mr. Dales, had been so moved with pity for the desperate man that he had offered him the use of his own rental house, free of charge, until Robber

Bob could get back on his feet. Mayor Chambers, owner of the A&P, also gave him a job at the grocery store.

The eleven-year-old identical Fuller triplets came in next. They were Connie Lynn, Sunny Gaye, and Bonnie Clare, whose flaxen hair and blue eyes could light up a dark room. They were street evangelists who sang in three-part harmony as fine as the famous Andrews Sisters.

Next came Reese Mullins with some of his brothers and sisters. Reese used to fancy himself Ruby's beau, but that was before Peter Reeder came to town and stole her heart away.

After the Mullins children, Ruby was in such a whirlwind of greetings and giggles that she couldn't keep up with who had come in and who wasn't there yet. Of course every kid who lived in town *would* come. That's the way it was in Way Down. When you threw a party, you didn't have to send out invitations. You just told a few people, or you mentioned it over your telephone party line, and everybody got the message. You saved a lot of time that way.

Just then Rita approached Ruby and hugged her around the waist.

"Happy birthday, Ruby."

Rita was wearing a cute green and white pokey-dotted dress that Ruby had outgrown when she was six.

Ruby hugged her back.

Miss Arbutus and Ruby both had taken a shine to the little girl, and Rita had been spending every school night at The Roost in the tiny pansy-speckled room next door to Miss Arbutus, which used to be Ruby's room.

"So we can give her a good breakfast every morning," Miss Arbutus had explained to Rita's daddy, when asking his permission to keep the child, "and dress her pretty for school."

Robber Bob had agreed. He was tickled to see his only daughter get some feminine attention, since her own mother had died almost a year ago. Rita had started first grade in September, and Ruby and Miss Arbutus helped her with her schoolwork. They also introduced the little girl to their evening ritual of grooming and the sharing of confidences. When they were finished, and darkness had settled over their town nestled way down deep between the mountains, Ruby and Miss Arbutus would kiss Rita good night and hug each other. Then Ruby would go up to the second floor to visit with Grandma for a few minutes and give her a good-night hug as well before retiring to her spacious pastel boudoir, which was right beside Grandma's room.

Each Friday when school let out, six-year-old Rita would walk to her own house, just a hop and a skip up the street from The Roost, to spend the weekend with her daddy, Robber Bob; her addled granddaddy, Bird; and her four brothers. At dusk on Sunday evening Ruby would fetch her back to The Roost. It was an arrangement quite satisfactory to everybody concerned.

"I got you a present," Rita said to Ruby as she handed the older girl a small package wrapped in brown paper.

Not everybody was able to give Ruby a gift, but she didn't mind a bit. Inside the paper was an odd pewter-colored metal button with a hole in it.

Ruby was delighted. "What an uncommon thing!" And it really was. It looked like it might have come from a soldier's uniform.

"You can put a ribbon through the hole, and make a pretty necklace," Rita said proudly.

"What a good idea!" Ruby cried. "Thank you, Rita."

Carefully Ruby placed the metal button inside a small pocket in her new dress. Then she hugged the beaming little girl again.

"Let's play blind man's bluff!" somebody yelled.

Yes, they should start the games. What a grand party this was going to be!

After blind man's bluff, they played guess what?, then treasure hunt. It was during this game that the party expanded outdoors, because Miss Arbutus and Grandma had hidden some of the treasures in the yard.

Ruby and Peter were seated side by side in the common room, watching Skeeter and Jeeter tussle over a piece of bubble gum they had found in a vase, when suddenly Slim Morgan charged through the front door.

"Catastrophe!" he yelled. "Where's Ruby at?"

"I'm here, Slim. What'sa matter?"

"It's Jethro, Ruby. I think he's dead."

2

WHEN RUBY WAS AROUND SEVEN YEARS OLD, A TRAVELER had offered a baby goat to Miss Arbutus in exchange for two hot meals and a room for the night. Ruby had named the animal Jethro, and he had been her pet ever since. He stayed in the yard outside The Roost, lived a comfortable life, and in fact became quite famous among the people of Way Down for his antics.

"Oh, dern, we'll never get to see him climb the woodpile again!" Skeeter Reeder wailed.

"And we'll never get to see him stand on the top of a car again!" Jeeter Reeder moaned.

"He'll never again run up to me when he sees my face at the back door," Ruby said, and burst into tears.

For it was true: this funny animal, belonging to Ruby but beloved by all the town, was indeed dead. He lay stretched out on his side in the autumn leaves, his tiny eyes closed, his white goatee full of chocolate, and his little goat heart at rest.

"Chocolate?" Miss Arbutus said. "Ohhh, chocolate. The poor

thing must have found the Hershey bar I hid on the porch for the treasure hunt."

"Do you think that's what killed him?" Lucy Elkins asked.

"If so, it's not a bad way to go," Grandma said.

The children gathered around Ruby and tried to comfort her.

"He was kinda dumb anyhow."

"Don't cry. It'll make your eyes red."

"A funeral! A funeral!" Connie Lynn Fuller cried.

"Yes, a funeral!" Sunny Gaye agreed.

"And *we* will officiate!" Bonnie Clare added.

"What's that?" Reese Mullins wanted to know.

"A funeral?" Connie Lynn said. "It's a ceremony for the dead before you bury them in the ground."

"I know what a funeral is!" Reese sputtered. "I mean what's off . . . off . . . ?"

"Officiate?" Bonnie Clare said. "It means we are in charge." And she waved a hand around to indicate herself and her sisters.

"It has to be a proper funeral," Ruby sobbed, and buried her face in Miss Arbutus's chest.

"Of course it must," Miss Arbutus said, as she patted Ruby's back. "We will bury him on that grassy spot beside the sign where the ground is nice and flat."

Everyone understood that Miss Arbutus was talking about the sign that read WAY UP THAT-A-WAY. It had an arrow on it pointing to the path that curled up the mountainside to the home of Granny Butler, the albino woman who had the gift of communication with animals.

"Yes, it's a sunny location," Ruby said, "and Jethro loved the sun."

Miss Arbutus found a shovel. All the kids went to the flat spot beside the sign and took turns digging a hole for Jethro's grave. Ruby was excused from that duty. The Mullins children—Reese, Mary Nell, Susie, Pauline, Junior, Clarence, and Gerry Joy—did the most digging, as they all had jobs at their family's two places of business, the Pure Gas Station and The Boxcar Grill, and were familiar with hard work. In fact, it was a rare Saturday that their parents gave them time off, but Ruby's birthday was special.

The Morgan children—Juanita, Jude, Edna, and Slim—were also a big help, and the Reeder boys did their share, while Rita tried to comfort Ruby. Soon they had a hole large enough for Jethro's poor lifeless body to fit into. The bigger boys carried the body to the grave.

"You can't just dump him into the dirt!" Ruby cried out. "He has to have a casket."

"You're absolutely right," Grandma said. "I've got just the thing."

When Grandma went into the house to fetch the thing that was "just the thing," the Fuller triplets started humming "Amazing Grace," and when she came back outside, they were in full harmony and volume, while others were trying to sing along, but not in the same key.

Grandma had brought out a big rectangular basket with a fitted lid that, she had once explained to Ruby, she had made from broom straw with her own hands when she was young. It was now too dilapidated to be of further use to Grandma but would be perfect for Jethro's needs. Grandma set the basket down on the ground and removed the lid. The boys picked up the goat by the legs and placed him gently into it. Everybody took a last look at Jethro. Except for his head being in an odd position so that he would fit into his casket, he seemed comfortable enough.

"O death, where is thy sting?" Connie Lynn quoted scripture.

"O grave, thou hast no victory." Sunny Gaye *mis*quoted scripture to make it more dramatic as Peter, Cedar, Reese, and Slim lowered the casket into the ground.

Ker-plump! One of the boys lost his grip and the basket fell unevenly into the hole. There was a scramble to upright it, and in the process Cedar fell in on top of the dead goat.

"**^##@++$!" Cedar let out a string of cuss words too appalling for human ears.

The shock of finding himself nose to nose with a dead thing had caused him to backslide on his resolve never to cuss again. The triplets clapped six hands over their six ears as there was another scramble to pull Cedar out of the hole. Cedar, of course, was more than mortified to have an attack of cussitis in the presence of the triplet angels. Since he could not tell one from the other, he was hopelessly in love with all three of them, and he knew how they deplored bad words.

"In my father's house," Bonnie Clare courageously continued with the service.

"There are many mansions," Connie Lynn finished the verse for her.

"And some of them are goat mansions," Sunny Gaye declared happily.

"Amen!" the triplets said together, then began to sing "Mansion on the Hilltop" as pretty as you please. It was among their top ten hits, and it suited the moment perfectly.

Peter dropped the basket lid down over poor Jethro, and there was nothing left to do but shovel the dirt back into the hole. Ruby did not care to see this part, so she turned away.

Rita pulled at Ruby's dress tail. "Now, can we have some cake?"

"I think we should," Ruby said. "Jethro would want us to."

On hearing the word *cake* the grave diggers went into overdrive and promptly finished the job. When all hands had been washed under the outside pump, the birthday cake was carried from the kitchen to the front porch. Everybody gathered around to see Ruby make her wish and blow out the candles. She closed her eyes and wished real, real hard. Then she took a big breath and blew out all thirteen candles in one tremendous puff.

3

RUBY HAD MET GRANDMA FOR THE FIRST TIME THIS PAST summer and had stayed with her on Yonder Mountain. While there, she had told Grandma stories not only about Jethro, her best friend Peter, and her other young friends but also about the folks living at The Roost and elsewhere in Way Down. Grandma had started to daydream, like a young girl, of living in that boardinghouse in that town, among those people. She had long ago given up ever having one of her dreams come true, but now here she was, and it was as good as she had imagined. Grandma had been living at The Roost for almost a month, and it had been the most excellent month of her life. She had never before had so much fun chatting and laughing with others.

Each morning she rose with the singing birds and scuttled down the stairs to help Miss Arbutus and Lucy Elkins fix breakfast. At one time, Ruby had been the only assistant in the kitchen. Now it seemed Miss Arbutus had more helpers than she really needed, but it was a nice break for Ruby. She was able to spend extra time preparing herself and Rita for school.

Grandma loved eating her meals around the big oak table with the other guests. After breakfast she would go out to the roomy wraparound porch, sit in one of the white rocking chairs, and holler out greetings to people as they walked by. Everybody in town was friendly to her. Some even stopped to talk. They all knew who she was, and by this time they knew her life story. They also knew that every Monday, Wednesday, and Friday afternoon Grandma walked down to the library where Mrs. Gentry, formerly Miss Worly, was teaching her to read and write, because in Grandma's day country girls were not properly educated. She had spent her entire life on one mountaintop or another until she had become as mean and ornery as a caged animal. The people in Way Down sympathized with her and admired her metamorphosis into this new and improved personality.

Another permanent guest at The Roost was Mr. A. H. Crawford, who lived on the third floor and was writing a book called *A Colorful History of Way Down Deep, West Virginia*. He, too, had recently changed into a new creature.

It was well-known that Mr. Crawford used to have the blues and had slept away a good bit of his life, but recently he had been up so early that he had time to go to the kitchen and aggravate the ladies as they prepared breakfast. They were too gracious to tell him to get out of the way, so they pretended he was a walking, talking piece of furniture and went around him.

After breakfast, Mr. Crawford retired to his room to write. When the weather was warm and the windows were open, you could hear his typewriter all up and down Ward Street. The townspeople thought of book writing as a highfalutin occupation that rather tickled their fancy.

"I wonder what fascinating words are flying onto the pages," they would say to themselves.

Or, "Is he writing about my ancestors?"

Or more often, "Am *I* in the book?"

But now that October's chill had crept into town, the doors and windows were shut tight and Mr. Crawford's typewriter could not be heard except by the residents of The Roost.

"Maybe you could let me peep at a few pages," Lucy Elkins said to Mr. Crawford in her thin, melodious voice. It was the Monday morning after Ruby's party, and she was setting the table for breakfast. "I don't think I can wait another day to read the book."

"And my reading lessons with Mrs. Gentry are coming along so well," Grandma chimed in, "that I may be able to read some of it myself."

"Now, ladies," Mr. Crawford said as he stood in the middle of the kitchen floor waving around an empty coffee cup, which Miss Arbutus finally refilled. "Please be patient. I will have finished the manuscript by Christmas, but I don't want anyone to read it until it has been made into a book."

He wouldn't admit even to himself how much he enjoyed these early-morning moments with the three ladies of the house. Since he had commenced writing his book in earnest, they had showed so much admiration for him that he felt like their knight in shining armor.

Just then Ruby and Rita entered the room spruced up for

school. They went straight to Miss Arbutus, who, with a smile, examined them, told them how lovely they were, and gave each one a kiss on the cheek.

"Go to the table now," she instructed the girls, then turned to Grandma and said, "Will you fetch our other guests?"

Grandma nodded and left the room. She walked into the common room, where two temporary boarders were having a cup of coffee while sharing a copy of *The Way Down Deep Daily*. These two gentlemen were the familiar circuit-riding preacher and a dandy from Charleston who was hawking *The Book of Knowledge*.

"Breakfast is served," Grandma said very politely.

When the two men came to the table, Ruby, Rita, and Mr. Crawford were seated already. Lucy set a pitcher of orange juice beside Ruby, who passed it around to the guests. Miss Arbutus placed a platter of sausages and bacon in the center of the table next to a bowl of eggs scrambled with peppers and onions. Grandma brought in a tray laden with honey, butter, marmalade, and cherry preserves. Lucy returned with a boat of gravy and a basket of biscuits, and breakfast was ready.

The ladies sat down and the preacher said grace. Then there was much chatter and laughter as the food disappeared. The meals at this table were usually pleasant and noisy. This morning was no exception.

"Ruby, I was sorry to hear about Jethro," the preacher sympathized with her. "He climbed on top of my station wagon one time."

"He was a silly old thing, wasn't he?" Ruby said with a sad kind of smile.

"And last summer he ate one of my Bibles," the preacher continued. "But I couldn't scold him, because he was literally filled with the word of God."

A ripple of laughter went around the table.

"We planted him in the ground like a seed," six-year-old Rita spoke up. "So I'm waiting for baby goats to sprout from the dirt."

Rita was surprised when everybody laughed again, but she just shrugged and dipped her bacon in marmalade. She thought she would never understand adults. They laughed at unfunny things all the time.

"What kind of school do you have here?" the salesman asked.

"A very nice school for all the grades," Ruby said. "It's across the road."

"And is it only for Way Down residents?"

"No, the coal miners' children are bused in from the hollers in the hills," Ruby said, "and the Shimpock children are bused in, too."

"And what, pray tell, are Shimpock children?" the salesman came back.

"They are the black kids who live out of town in a small neighborhood called Shimpock," Ruby explained.

"Shimpock has a chapter in my book," Mr. Crawford interjected. "Only a dozen or so families live there. They used to have their own school, which, as you well know, is the custom in this part of the country. But their school was damaged by fire a few years back, and the people of Way Down invited the children of Shimpock to come here to be educated."

"How extraordinary," the salesman said thoughtfully. "And does this integrated school have *The Book of Knowledge* in every classroom?"

"No, sir, we don't," Ruby said. "We have only one set that we pass around from room to room."

"And do you have a library?"

"Not at the school, but there's one in town for everybody," Ruby replied.

"What a shame," the salesman said, "but you certainly should have more than one set of the wonderful *Book of Knowledge*."

"You must speak to the principal," Mr. Crawford went on. "His name is Mr. Bear, and he's quite a pleasant fellow."

"And Mrs. Gentry is the town librarian," Lucy Elkins spoke up. "You should speak to her as well."

The salesman took a pad and a pen from the pocket of his imitation gabardine jacket and jotted down the two names.

"And are all the students as well bred as these two?" the salesman asked, smiling at Ruby and Rita.

"You'll find the children of Way Down are treasures," Miss Arbutus spoke up, which was a small surprise, because she did not often contribute to conversations at the table.

Her remark reminded Grandma of a favorite subject.

"Have you, by chance, sir, heard the legend of the treasure of Way Down Deep?" she asked the salesman.

"I can't say that I have," he replied.

"Then please let me tell it to you," Grandma said excitedly.

It was one of the stories Ruby had told her during the summer, and Grandma had been dying to repeat it to somebody who hadn't heard of it. Such a person had been nonexistent until now.

"You see, the founder of this town was a man by the name of Archibald Ward," Grandma began. "And word has been handed down through the generations that he brought a treasure to Way Down those many years ago. People say he found a pirate's booty during one of his explorations on the coast of Virginia. Gold doubloons and pieces of eight. But he never spent the money because he was afraid the pirates would find him and kill him. So he buried it here, far from the coast and the prying eyes of the world."

"And have people searched for it over the years?" the salesman asked.

"Oh, yes, but without success. You see it was buried way down deep somewhere here in Way Down Deep. But nobody knows where."

4

ON THE SCHOOL PLAYGROUND THAT MORNING RUBY JOINED Peter, who stood chatting with a small group of other classmates, including Johnny Ray Springstep. Johnny Ray lived in Black Snake Holler, about ten miles out of town. He was a towheaded kid with sky-blue eyes and a dimple in each cheek. His pa was a coal miner, and so were his two older brothers and two uncles on his ma's side, but he was going to be a doctor. He had made that decision when he was ten years old. At that time an epidemic of flu was running rampant throughout Black Snake Holler, and Johnny Ray was the only member of his family left standing on his feet.

Not knowing how to tend his loved ones, he had sought the advice of a very old mountain medicine woman, and she had told him to make a strong tea of elderberries and ginger. So Johnny Ray brewed a batch of the stuff, and gave it first of all to his pa and ma, then to each of his five siblings. In no time they all began to sweat liberally and throw back their quilts. In a matter of hours the entire Springstep household was well enough to help Johnny Ray prepare the tea for neighbors and relatives. The warmth and satisfaction he had felt in making sick people well got into his blood like a virus unto itself. He vowed to become a real honest-to-God doctor, then come back to the hills and minister to his own people. That ambition, along with a sharp mind and a curiosity that would kill a whole slew of cats, drove Johnny Ray Springstep to be among the best students at the Way Down school. His teachers—except for one—had always said so.

Of course all the chatter in the school yard was of Ruby's birthday party and the untimely demise of poor Jethro. The holler kids and the Shimpock kids listened with great interest, for they had often seen Jethro across the street climbing the woodpile or standing on the top of somebody's car. Also, birthday parties were not common events in their world. Sometimes they felt lucky just to get an extra hug on their birthday.

"What color was the cake icing?" Johnny Ray wanted to know.

"It was yellow," Ruby said, "with white frosty letters."

"And what was on the inside of it?" Becky Trueheart, a small pretty black girl from Shimpock asked. Ruby looked at her and felt a pang of pity, for she could see the poor kid's mouth was watering at the mere description of cake. Ruby had always thought it a shame that the Shimpock children and the holler children got left out of many activities because they lived so far out of town.

Ruby took Becky's arm, nudged her away from the others, and whispered into her ear, "It's lemon, and I have a piece for you in my book bag. I don't have one for everybody, so you can't tell."

Becky's cinnamon eyes radiated excitement. "I won't tell."

"I'll give it to you at morning break," Ruby whispered again, and giggling together over their secret, the two girls rejoined the group.

At that moment an old blue Buick pulled into the school yard and parked. A woman got out of the car and walked toward a side door of the building without looking right or left. She had shoulder-length brown hair and was dressed in a plain brown frock. Although she was young in years she somehow gave the impression of a disgruntled little old lady. In a moment she had vanished inside.

"Oooo," Cedar Reeder said, and wrinkled his nose like he smelled something icky.

"Oooo what?" Ruby said, but everybody knew what.

"Miss Puke," Cedar said.

"Don't call her that!" Ruby said. "Miss *Duke* is our teacher. Have some respect."

"Respect!" Reese popped into the conversation. "How can you respect a grumpy old grouch like her?"

It was true that Miss Duke, the new English teacher for all the seventh and eighth graders, was about as popular as a tax collector. She had arrived in town on Kids' Day, which was a special day set aside by the mayor to celebrate and honor all the kids in Way Down. Not seeming to care what was going on, Miss Duke had driven her dilapidated Buick right smack dab through the middle of the parade on Busy Street.

She had accepted the job at the Way Down school with reluctance because she perceived the town to be backward. However, she was smart enough to know that a first-year teacher could not afford to be choosy and that she should consider herself lucky to find any position at all.

In searching for a place to live, she had visited The Roost, where Miss Arbutus had offered her a room at a discount, but Miss Duke had turned up her nose at it, explaining in her Yankee accent that she did not like the idea of taking her meals with the locals. Instead, she moved into a two-room apartment over the garage in Mayor Chambers's fine house out on Highway 99. She appeared at the school in her car every morning with a frown on her face, then disappeared again every afternoon with a deeper frown. Nobody caught a glimpse of her at any other time, except perchance as she shopped. For a young person, she was not sociable at all.

From the first day of school Johnny Ray Springstep and Miss Duke had been at odds with each other. Maybe it was because he could no more stop his mouth from running than a skunk could stop stinking. And that seemed to annoy Miss Duke no end. Or maybe it was because she was as ordinary-looking as a mud fence, while Johnny Ray was almost as cute as Peter Reeder. Or could it be that she had always dreamed of escaping a Pennsylvania coal-mining town only to find herself in a West Virginia coal-mining town, and Johnny Ray, the smart kid from a mining family, somehow represented her sense of hopelessness? Whatever the reason, it seemed like she had made up her mind that he was a troublemaker, and he had made up his mind that she was the awfullest teacher that ever was.

Cedar Reeder found Miss Duke intimidating. His knee-jerk reaction was to call her unflattering names—behind her back, of course. When he had done such a thing at home one night, his dad, Robber Bob, had stretched himself up to his full five feet of height and declared, "I will not have any son of mine making fun of his teacher! You heah me?"

But after parents' night, when Robber Bob had met Miss Duke, he had come home with his own opinion of the teacher. He just couldn't express it in the presence of children.

"She's not from here," Miss Arbutus had told Ruby.

That was explanation enough for most residents of Way Down—she was from elsewhere.

"And we don't know what kind of life she's had," Miss Arbutus had continued. "So as long as you are in her class, you will treat her with kindness and respect."

Actually, Ruby had saved that nice slice of cake for Miss Duke because, no matter how she felt about that unpleasant person, she had wanted to at least try to be kind, as Miss Arbutus had advised. But on seeing poor Becky Trueheart salivating over the mere description of birthday cake, Ruby had resolved that her heart was not in the giving of a gift to Miss Duke. Becky was a different story.

Becky was a sweet, smart girl who wanted to be a teacher herself someday. She made straight A's all the time and helped her little brothers and sisters with their homework every night. She even played school with the Shimpock children in the summertime—whether they wanted to or not. She always took the role of teacher in preparation for the day when she would stand before a real class. It was a sweet dream. But her daddy, an uneducated man himself, was the street sweeper in Way Down and had never in his life had more than five dollars tucked away for a rainy day.

Throughout Miss Duke's second-period English class, Becky shot glances at Ruby, who sat two desks behind her. Ruby would give her a conspiratorial smile, and Becky would look at the clock on the wall. Thirty minutes till break. Twenty minutes till break.

"Johnny Ray Springstep! Stop talking!" Miss Duke suddenly bellowed.

Becky, who sat in the front row, was so startled at this outburst that she jumped inches out of her desk. The class was supposed to be working quietly on verb conjugation while the teacher was grading papers at her desk. At the moment Miss Duke was wearing her green cat-eye reading glasses, which made her look even meaner than she was.

Finding himself being yelled at once again in the presence of the class, of which many were pretty girls, Johnny Ray felt his face burn, and he bent low over his work. Fifteen minutes till break. Silence again lay over the classroom. Only the scratching of pencils on paper could be heard.

"All right, put your pencils down," Miss Duke directed. "Who will go first?"

Becky raised her hand.

"And what verb did you choose to conjugate, Becky?"

"To sing," Becky replied, then stood up and recited what she had done.

> "I sing. You sing. He sings. We sing. Y'all sing. They sing . . . I sang. You sang. He sang. We sang. Y'all sang. They sang . . . I will sing. You will sing. He will sing. We will sing. Y'all will sing. They will sing."

"Right," Miss Duke said when Becky was finished, "except that I have told you before that *y'all* is not a proper pronoun."

"Oh, but in West Virginia it is, Miss Duke," Becky blurted out.

Miss Duke glared at her and said, "No, Becky Trueheart, *y'all* is never a proper pronoun anyplace, anytime, anyhow!"

Becky wanted to push her point further by informing Miss Duke that *y'all* was a perfectly good pronoun when referring to more than one person, and that its use added a bit of charm to the otherwise sluggish Southern accent. Yes indeed, Becky *did* think that and was truly able to express herself in those terms, given a little support. But instead she slid back into her seat and said no more, while at the same time promising herself that when she became a teacher she would never demoralize a student like that.

"Johnny Ray," Miss Duke said. "What verb did you do?"

Johnny Ray did not respond.

"Johnny Ray Springstep!" Miss Duke raised her voice.

Johnny Ray stood up beside his desk but still did not speak.

"Well?" Miss Duke said sharply.

Johnny Ray said nothing.

"Did you conjugate a verb or not?"

Johnny Ray bobbed his head up and down.

"Then let's hear it!" Miss Duke cried.

"You told me not to talk," Johnny Ray said, then slammed his mouth shut again.

"Talk!" Miss Duke said angrily. "Now!"

That's when Johnny Ray exploded. "One minute you holler at me for talking, and the next minute you holler at me for *not* talking. So which is it?"

There was stunned silence in the room as Johnny Ray's classmates looked with rounded eyes from him to the teacher. Miss Duke's jawline was so tight you might think she had a fatal case of lockjaw.

"Go to Mr. Bear's office," she hissed at Johnny Ray through her clenched teeth, "and do not dawdle on the way."

The principal was not even half as scary as the teacher, so Johnny Ray immediately took her up on her offer. He was out of the classroom before the second hand on the clock could move again.

"Slim Morgan." Miss Duke calmly went on with the lesson. "What's your verb?"

Slim stood up with a smile on his face. He was as good-natured a boy as you would find anywhere.

"To puke," Slim said happily. "I puke. You puke. He pukes—"

To everybody's relief the break bell rang.

5

I T SO HAPPENED THAT THE FIVE BRIGHTEST MEMBERS OF THE senior class—two girls and three boys—met in Mr. Bear's office every Monday and Wednesday morning for instruction in chemistry, because the principal was the only one at the school qualified to teach the subject. The rest of the week the small class did independent study in a makeshift science lab in the basement of the building, where they performed their chemistry experiments and discussed lofty notions that were way over the heads of regular people.

On that morning, as the break bell rang for the middle grades, Johnny Ray stepped into Mr. Bear's office. The principal motioned for him to sit in a chair beside the *Book of Knowledge* salesman.

"Sorry," Mr. Bear apologized to Johnny Ray, as he had earlier done with the salesman. "I have to do a little teaching here, and I'll be with y'all in a jiffy."

Then he went back to what he was saying to his class.

As Johnny Ray listened to Mr. Bear teaching, it was like

fireworks going off in his head. He didn't even know what this class was called, but somehow he understood the material and found it engrossing.

To digress briefly, Johnny Ray had gone back many times to learn as much as he could from the old medicine woman who had taught him how to heal with herb tea. He felt that her old-timey remedies should be used alongside the latest scientific discoveries, because he was sure that each had a place in the healing arts. She had discussed with him some of the secrets of the ages, such as synchronicity, which is a fancy word meaning that when one is on the right path through life, all things work together to bring about the circumstances one needs to fulfill one's destiny. So here was the reason, Johnny Ray thought, that he had chosen this particular morning to sass Miss Duke. He was meant to be sent to the principal's office for the purpose of being introduced to the preliminaries of his future studies.

"In trouble with your teacher?" the salesman whispered to Johnny Ray.

"Uh-huh," Johnny Ray mumbled without missing a word of Mr. Bear's instruction.

"That's how it was with me in school," the salesman said with a chuckle. "I've still done all right for myself. How old are you, boy?"

But Johnny Ray did not hear the question. He was captivated by chemistry.

"What do you want to be when you grow up?"

Johnny Ray did not respond.

"You could be a salesman like me. There's a pretty good living in encyclopedias, though you have to travel a lot and be away from your family."

At this point Mr. Bear glanced over and was surprised to see that it was the salesman who was whispering instead of Johnny Ray. He did not want to embarrass a grown-up by telling him to be quiet, so he simply turned up the volume of his lecture.

"A doctor," Johnny Ray finally whispered to the salesman.

"You want to be a doctor?" the salesman said out loud.

"Shhhhh," Johnny Ray said.

"Okay," Mr. Bear was saying to the five seniors. "Do exercises three and four; then let me check your work."

With those words the principal turned again to Johnny Ray and the salesman. "We must speak quietly while they do their assignment."

"Of course," the salesman said softly.

"Can I take this class?" Johnny Ray blurted out.

"Yes, when you're a senior," Mr. Bear answered.

"I want to take it now," Johnny Ray insisted.

Two of the seniors glanced up and smiled condescendingly. Imagine Johnny Ray Springstep thinking he could study chemistry.

"Let's step out here for a moment," Mr. Bear said patiently to his visitors as he ushered them through the door. Johnny Ray moved with reluctance and looked back over his shoulder at the class.

The *out here* referred to by the principal was the front hallway, where there was a desk and a chair. Mrs. Bevins, the barber's wife, was stationed there that day as a volunteer for the purpose of answering the telephone and performing other miscellaneous duties that a paid secretary would have done if the school budget had allowed for such a luxury.

Always the spiffy dresser, Mrs. Bevins wore her October suit of gold and green, a pair of brown shoes, and a hat busily decorated in red and orange plastic leaves.

Mr. Bear turned to the salesman, with the expectation of hearing why he was there, but the salesman deferred to Johnny Ray, saying, "You go first, sonny."

Johnny Ray seemed bewildered, as his reason for being there had momentarily slipped his mind.

"Oh," he said directly. "Miss Duke sent me. I talked."

Mr. Bear sighed. "You talked?"

"Yes, sir. I mean I talked back to her. I shouldn'ta done it."

"Indeed. Just go to my office and wait for me, Johnny Ray. I'll take care of you in a minute."

"Yes, sir!" Johnny Ray said happily, and hurried into the principal's office, where the chemistry class was busy with exercises three and four.

Mr. Bear gave his attention to the salesman, feeling grumpy and a bit put upon. "And what can I do for you?"

"That boy thinks he's going to be a doctor!" the salesman said, and laughed out loud. "He has no idea!"

Mrs. Bevins's crinolines rustled as she changed positions in her chair and waited to hear Mr. Bear's retort. Everybody knew that Mr. Bear would not listen to disparaging remarks about his "cubs."

Mr. Bear said nothing, however, but merely glared at the salesman.

"Oh, sorry," the salesman said, and came quickly to the point. "I am here, sir, to offer you an educator's discount for the wonderful *Book of Knowledge*. I understand that you have only one set in your whole school."

Whereupon the salesman opened a briefcase and proceeded to do his pitch right then and there in the hallway. Mrs. Bevins watched and listened, wondering when Mr. Bear was going to toss the man out on his rear end. But Mr. Bear surprised her.

"I'll take two sets," he said when the salesman stopped to take a breath. "The set we have is ten years old, so we've needed them for some time."

The salesman's mouth was left hanging open as Mr. Bear said to Mrs. Bevins, "Would you take care of this order, please?"

"Yes, sir," Mrs. Bevins replied.

"Take the money from the textbook fund," Mr. Bear said to her. "We'll try to make it up with a bake sale . . . or something." He turned to the salesman and gave his hand a quick shake. "Good day to you."

Then he left abruptly to go back into his office/classroom. There, to his amazement, he found Johnny Ray had fallen head over heels into a discussion with the seniors. In fact, the boy was peppering them with such intelligent questions that they were too startled to do anything but reply in a like manner, as if Johnny Ray were an equal.

Mr. Bear, who was a religious man, was reminded of the twelve-year-old Jesus conferring with the learned scribes in the temple. And all his grumpiness fell away. In fact, his heart was filled with pride, because he had always considered Johnny Ray one of his prize cubs.

Yes, his job sometimes was so demanding that he had to go away by himself and pray. But at times like this he knew beyond a doubt he was doing something right, no matter how hard it was.

Who said Johnny Ray Springstep would never be a doctor?

6

A FEW NIGHTS LATER, AFTER SAYING GOOD NIGHT TO EVERY-body, Ruby looked out her bedroom window toward the sign that read WAY UP THAT-A-WAY, near which they had buried poor Jethro. In the dark she could barely make out the grave, but when she had watched for only a matter of seconds, sure enough there came Jethro's shadow prancing around in the grass. It had been there each night since his burial.

Ruby mourned for her pet more than anybody knew. He had been her friend for six years, and she could hardly remember the time before he came. His loss had also made her think more deeply about life and death, and the fact that all of us must die, animal and human alike. Her mother and father already had died. Miss Arbutus would also die someday. How awful that would be. Her most special friend, Peter Reeder, would die. And what about Grandma? She would die sooner than any of them. Of course, Ruby would die, too. She couldn't quite absorb that part. So what was this dark, mysterious thing called death? Where did it take you?

In attending the various churches in Way Down, Ruby had been taught that the body goes back to dust, but the spirit goes to heaven or hell, depending on one's behavior throughout life. Ruby could not imagine those places. So she made up her own afterlife. It was a place exactly like Way Down Deep, for what could be better? She had grown up feeling like a vital part of this town, like one of the beats in its heart.

"Good night, my friend," she whispered to Jethro with a sigh, and wiped tears from her eyes. "I miss you."

Ruby did not think it unusual to see Jethro's shadow by his grave. She had never questioned the possibility of ghosts or of any other mystical goings-on. She thought Miss Arbutus attracted such things to The Roost.

Miss Arbutus's dreams, for example, were legendary. She actually left her body and went places when she was asleep. To England one time. To a volcano once when she was a girl with a fever. Then one special moonlit night Miss Arbutus had dreamed of rescuing a toddler from a sad situation on a mountaintop, and early the next morning two-and-a-half-year-old Ruby had appeared in town wearing her petticoat. Only this past summer had the townspeople learned that Ruby had been carried from her grandma's house on Yonder Mountain, sixty miles away, to Way Down by Miss Arbutus in her dream.

Ruby turned off the lamp beside her bed and crawled under the covers. She loved her sheets, which were clean and crisp and as purple as amethyst. She could barely hear Mr. Crawford's typewriter *tap, tap, tapping* from his room above hers. It was a comforting sound and soon tapped her to sleep.

Late in the night she woke up and lay listening, but there was no sound at this hour. No typewriter, no cars, nothing. She tiptoed to the window in the dark and looked for Jethro's shadow, but it seemed that he had also gone to sleep.

Her mouth and throat felt parched, and she reckoned that was the reason she woke up. She would go down to the kitchen for a glass of water. She snapped on the lamp and dressed in her robe and slippers, because the house was chilly at night. She went into the hallway and listened. From the room beside hers, she could hear Grandma snoring, but there was no sound from Lucy Elkins's room across the hall, nor from the third floor where the male boarders were sleeping. That night they included the preacher, Mr. Crawford, and Mr. Elbert Deel, the traveling judge who came to hold court in Way Down once a month. The *Book of Knowledge* salesman had moved on after failing to sell a set of his encylopedias to the library. Mrs. Gentry had been sorry to inform him that her budget would not allow anything new right now.

The stairs were lit with two dim electric lanterns on the wall. Ruby scuttled down the steps and into the kitchen, where she snapped on another light over the sink. In its glow she could see Miss Arbutus standing at the open back door, dressed only in a long white nightgown, looking out at the night as if she were in a trance. A chilling October breeze seemed to pass right through her and into the room.

"Miss Arbutus!" Ruby said. "You'll catch your death!"

Miss Arbutus turned toward Ruby and smiled.

"Everything okay?" Ruby asked as she quickly closed the

door and leaned her back against it, looking at Miss Arbutus's face.

"I had a dream," Miss Arbutus said.

"A good one?"

"I think so. It was strange."

Ruby went to the cabinet, took a glass, and filled it with water from the kitchen tap. There was a step stool in the pantry, so she pulled it out into the middle of the room and perched upon it.

"I was in front of Granny Butler's cabin," Miss Arbutus said. "I don't remember climbing the hill, but suddenly I was there, and Granny Butler's animals were milling about. I know they always talk to her, and tonight they talked to me as well."

"What did they say?"

"They said all kinds of things. They told me where to find the best hickory-nut trees. They said Granny Butler's pumpkins are bigger than anybody else's this year. They updated me on the health of Aristotle the owl, who has arthritis in one wing. A raccoon asked me why animals can't trick-or-treat at Halloween.

"Then there was this red fox named Ripple," Miss Arbutus continued, "and he told me he had heard about my night on Yonder Mountain from his old foxy grandpappy. Those were his words."

"And then what happened?" Ruby asked.

"Well, I didn't know what I was doing up there, and I certainly didn't want to wake up Granny Butler with all that chatter, so I started back home."

"But how could you wake her up? You were in a dream, weren't you?" Ruby said.

"Yes, but you know as well as anybody that sometimes my dreams spill over into reality. Or maybe reality spills into my dreams."

There was silence in the room for a moment.

"Anyway, it's a lovely night for a stroll," Miss Arbutus went on, "so I walked down the mountain. I was in my nightgown, but I wasn't at all cold. I was enjoying the beauty around me when all of a sudden there was Jethro standing by the path like he was waiting for me."

"For real?"

"For real," Miss Arbutus said, "and the first words out of his mouth were, 'Tell Ruby not to be sad. Tell her I'm happy.'"

Instantly the thought occurred to Ruby that Miss Arbutus was making this up to lift her spirits.

"He could talk, too?" Ruby asked.

"Sure he could. And he said that he knows you are watching him when he prances around the sign at night. That funny goat always did like to show off."

No way Miss Arbutus could have made up that part, for Ruby had told nobody about seeing Jethro's shadow.

"He does it to cheer you up," Miss Arbutus said. "And he told me one more thing. He said a stranger will make your birthday wish come true."

"*My* birthday wish?" Ruby sputtered.

"That's what he said. A stranger will make Ruby's birthday wish come true."

"Wow!" Ruby said. "How would a dead goat know a thing like that?"

Miss Arbutus chuckled. "It was only a dream, Ruby."

"But it was *your* dream," Ruby said, "and that makes it special. You have a gift for knowing and seeing and hearing things that the rest of us don't have. That's why Jethro talks to you instead of me."

"What did you wish for?" Miss Arbutus asked.

"I'm not supposed to tell—but it seems so unlikely, it's probably okay. I wished to find the treasure of Way Down Deep."

"Well, it's a nice thought," Miss Arbutus said.

Ruby finished her water and walked to the sink. Just as she was placing her empty glass inside it, she was startled by a dreadful racket behind her. She whirled around to find Grandma in her nightgown sprawled across the step stool, which she had obviously stumbled over.

"Heck!" Grandma exclaimed. (Or it's possible that she used a stronger expletive.)

"Oh, Grandma! I'm sorry!" Ruby cried, and helped the older woman to her feet.

"What's this stool doing here in the middle of the floor?" Grandma sputtered as she pulled herself together.

"It's my fault," Ruby said. "I was sitting on it. Are you hurt?"

"Only my pride. But why were you sitting here in the middle of the kitchen all by yourself?"

"I'm not by myself. Miss Arbutus is here."

When she turned to the back door, however, where Miss Arbutus had been standing, nobody was there.

"Miss Arbutus?" Grandma said. "Where?"

Ruby glanced around the room. Indeed, nobody else was there but Grandma.

"Didn't you see her?" she asked.

"No, but I didn't see that stool either," Grandma replied, rubbing her shins.

Ruby pushed the red curls away from her face and looked around the room again. What had just happened?

Then she knew. She had come upon Miss Arbutus while she was still in her dream! That could explain why the open door had not chilled her. The clatter of Grandma falling over the stool had jarred Miss Arbutus awake. So Miss Arbutus's physical body probably had never left her bed! With a thrill, Ruby realized that once again, just as on that long-ago night on Yonder Mountain when Miss Arbutus had rescued her, she had been in communication with Miss Arbutus's dream spirit.

7

SATURDAY, OCTOBER 9, WAS A CLEAR, COOL DAY. RUBY'S grandma, with her reading glasses perched on her nose, wore a thick sweater as she sat on the porch that afternoon scrutinizing a copy of *The Way Down Deep Daily*. Ever since she had started her reading lessons, she had been trying to read the newspaper for herself. Not only was it good practice, but it helped her to become better acquainted with the town. She found much of the paper was a challenge, but the classified ads were short and had easy words. They made her feel that she had accomplished a lot by figuring out what they said.

"Is Ruby here?" someone said, interrupting her concentration.

Grandma peered up over her glasses to find Peter on the steps holding a small white dog in his arms. Cedar was right behind him.

"She's in the kitchen helping Miss Arbutus carve a jack-o'-lantern," Grandma said. "During the night somebody dropped off the world's biggest pumpkin right here on the porch. Can I help you?"

"This dog came wandering into our yard," Peter said. "He seems to be lost, and he's hurt."

"We thought Ruby might want him," Cedar added.

"You thought that, did'ja?" Grandma said as she took off her reading glasses to take a closer look at the dog. She did not seem impressed. "What made you think Ruby would want an injured dog?"

Then she stood up and clomped inside, shutting the door behind her.

Peter and Cedar looked at the closed door with puzzled eyes.

"Do we stink or something?" Cedar asked.

"I took a bath only last week, didn't you?" Peter joked.

Before Cedar could respond, Grandma was back.

"Ruby'll be out in a jiffy," she said. "I didn't tell her about the mutt."

Peter and Cedar each chose one of the white rocking chairs and sat down with Grandma to wait for Ruby. Peter cuddled the dog and whispered to him.

"Let me show you how good I'm learning to read," Grandma said, and began to go through the help wanted ads aloud. She had already read them to herself, so the words came easy. The boys listened politely.

"Whoa!" Grandma interrupted herself suddenly, as a light-bulb came on in her head. "Before you offer that dog to Ruby," she said, "we should check the lost and found ads."

Peter and Cedar cut their eyes at each other. They were earnestly hoping that nobody had lost the dog or wanted to find him. They had fallen in love with him and would have kept him for themselves, but Robber Bob had told them that if the dog moved in, one of them would have to move out. They interpreted that to mean no.

Painstakingly, Grandma waded through the different ads until she came to the section she needed.

"Lost," she read at last. "Dog 3 mos. Uh, what's a mos?"

"It means months," Peter said, thinking that was approximately the age of this dog. "Three months old. What else does it say?"

The two boys held their breath while Grandma found her place again.

"White," she read.

Peter pulled the animal closer to him.

"And black," Grandma finished.

Peter and Cedar grinned.

"Can't be him," Cedar declared. "This dog is white all over. Except he's pink inside his ears, like puppies are, and on his tummy, too."

"Hey, Peter, Cedar," Ruby said as she came out the door. "Whose dog?"

Peter held the small bundle out toward Ruby. "Ain't he cute?"

The dog whimpered as Ruby took him into her arms. "Is he hurt?"

"Yeah, his leg's all messed up," Peter said.

"We found him," Cedar said. "Do you like him?"

"Yes, I love him. Are you going to keep him?"

"Well, we thought maybe you'd want him," Peter said, "since you don't have a pet anymore."

"Really?" Ruby said. "You want to give him to me?"

Ruby set the puppy down on the porch. With pitiful brown eyes he looked from her to Peter, then hobbled back to her.

Ruby's face lit up. "Did you see that?" She gently took him back into her arms. "He knows me already."

"It's that left hind leg," Peter said. "It's hurt bad."

"We should take him to see Mr. Doctor," Cedar said. "Don't you reckon?"

"But it's Saturday," Peter said. "Will he be in?"

"He's there most Saturdays," Ruby said, "but he's not an animal doctor."

"Yeah, but this is like an emergency, ain't it?" Cedar said.

"I suppose it is," Ruby said.

"Let's go, then," Peter said.

They were down the steps before Ruby remembered to turn back to Grandma and say, "Please tell Miss Arbutus that I'm going into town with Peter and Cedar."

Grandma grunted.

"And don't tell her anything else," Ruby added. "Please?"

Grandma grunted again, but Ruby stood her ground and waited for an answer.

"All right! All right!" Grandma agreed at last. "My lips are sealed."

The medical center was located on Busy Street beside the bank. In the right side of the building, Mr. Doctor took care of sick people, and in the left side there was a dentist's office where his wife, Mrs. Doctor, took care of people's teeth. Their last name was Justus, but nobody ever called them by it, because it would be confusing to have two Dr. Justuses.

There was a waiting room between the two offices, which on that day was empty except for Mr. Doctor taking a nap in one of the chairs, with his hands resting comfortably over his ample tummy. The arrival of three noisy kids did not wake him. Mrs. Doctor was nowhere to be seen, and there was no sound from her office.

Ruby coughed. Still Mr. Doctor slept on, moving his breath in and out heavily. His glasses had slid down to the end of his nose.

Ruby, Peter, and Cedar looked at one another and smiled.

"Wonder if the doctor's in!" Cedar yelled, and banged on the door they had just entered.

Mr. Doctor did not wake up.

"Yeah, this might be an emergency!" Peter hollered.

No luck.

Finally Ruby placed one small hand on the doctor's shoulder and shook it gently.

"What!" Mr. Doctor cried, and grabbed at his glasses as they fell onto his chest.

"It's just us," Ruby said.

"Who?" the doctor said as he stuck the glasses in place and peered at the kids through them. "What's going on here?"

"We brought you a patient," Ruby said.

"Where?" He looked the kids over. "Is somebody hurt?"

Ruby presented the dog.

"A canine?" Mr. Doctor snorted with contempt. "I don't take care of canines!"

"But he's hurt," Ruby said, "and we don't know what to do for him." She poked out her lower lip. She wondered if she should try to cry a bit. "He's so little."

The doctor was quiet as he looked at the kids and the dog. Finally, he stood up and said, "What seems to be wrong with him?"

"It's his left hind leg," Peter said.

Mr. Doctor placed his hands on his hips. "What this town needs is a good veterinarian."

"Yeah," Peter said. "That's what I'm gonna be."

Actually, the thought had never before entered Peter's head, but at that moment it seemed like such a good idea, he had to express it.

"I thought you was gonna be a drummer," Cedar said. "That's what you told Mr. Gentry."

"I'm gonna be a drummer, too. But most of all I want to be a vetin . . . an animal doctor."

"Huh!" Mr. Doctor said. "Do you now?"

"Yes, sir. I love animals."

"Well then, here's your first patient. You can use my examining room. Bring him along."

"Oh, thank you!" Peter said as he took the dog from Ruby.

Cedar and Ruby started to follow Peter and Mr. Doctor, but the doctor turned to them and said, "The vet needs only one assistant, and that's me. So shoo!"

Then he disappeared into his examining room with Peter and the dog. Ruby and Cedar sat down again to wait.

A few minutes later Peter came out again. "It looks like I'm going to have to operate," he said in a very official-sounding voice. "Y'all go on home."

"*You* are going to operate?" Ruby said.

"Well, yeah, sorta. Me and Mr. Doctor."

"You won't hurt my dog, will you?"

"Doc's got something to put him to sleep during the operation," Peter said, and patted Ruby on the shoulder. "Go on now. I'll let you know."

Then Peter disappeared again behind the closed door.

Two hours later, when supper was over and the kitchen cleaned, Ruby was sitting in the common room with Grandma, Lucy Elkins, and Mr. Crawford, while the three adults listened to the *Grand Ole Opry* on the radio. Ruby tried to listen, too. She managed to laugh when the others laughed, and she commented on the singing, but she was, as the peculiar expression goes, beside herself. She couldn't help fretting about the poor little white pup. What was taking so long?

When the front door opened, she leapt to her feet, and Peter came in carrying the dog wrapped in a white blanket.

"What's the verdict?" Ruby asked.

"Good news and bad news," Peter said. "Which one you want first?"

"Good news."

"He's gonna be fine—in time," Peter said, and pulled back the blanket to reveal the sleeping face.

"And the bad news?" Ruby said, and crossed her fingers.

"We had to remove most of that leg," Peter said. "We tried to save it, but it was in real bad shape. Mr. Doctor said he couldn't tell what might have happened to it."

"Three legs is not so bad," Ruby said as she took the pup from Peter and cuddled him against her heart. "It's one more than I've got."

"What's this?" Miss Arbutus said as she came in from the kitchen, where she had been checking supplies and writing a grocery list. "A dog?"

Ruby looked from face to face, but everybody was looking at *her*.

"Oh, I see how it is," Mr. Crawford said, breaking the silence. "I picked up a stray one time and sneaked him into my room. My mother was not pleased, to say the least."

"I wouldn't do that!" Ruby sputtered. "I would ask first." Then she seemed to have run out of words.

It so happened that when Miss Arbutus was a girl she had owned a dog whom she called Stinky. She had been so distressed when Stinky died that she had vowed never to become attached to another dog. But now, seeing Ruby cuddling the sleeping puppy, she was moved in her heart.

"You know he has to stay outside," she said to Ruby. "He'll bring in fleas. We can't run a boardinghouse with fleas in it."

She expected Ruby to fly into her arms and say, "Thank you,

thank you," but she was wrong. Ruby just stood there, looking wounded.

"Outside? In the cold?" she said.

"He can have Jethro's quilts on the back porch. He'll be all right."

"But he's hurt," Ruby went on. "Doc had to take off most of one leg."

"Hurt?" Miss Arbutus exclaimed, and with a big sigh sank down on the couch. "Ruby, how are you going to care for an injured animal and go to school, too?"

Grandma changed positions and mumbled something unintelligible.

"What did you say?" Ruby asked her grandma hopefully.

"I said maybe . . . Oh, I don't know . . ." Grandma said, then shifted her weight again and looked at the floor. "Maybe I can look after the dadblamed critter when you're in school," she finished quickly.

"And maybe I'll step in when you're gone for your reading lessons," Lucy Elkins said to Grandma.

Miss Arbutus sighed again, looking from Peter's anxious face to Ruby's.

"But he really will have to stay indoors till he's well again," Ruby persisted. "I'll fix him a place in my room. Please? Just for the winter?"

"And what about the fleas?" Miss Arbutus reminded her.

"We got two new sets of *The Book of Knowledge* at school," Peter interjected, "so I'll study up on fleas and find out what's the best thing in the world to keep them away."

They could see that Miss Arbutus was relenting. Her eyes were smiling. Ruby went to her and hugged her with one arm while holding the puppy in the other.

"Oh, thank you, Miss Arbutus," she said. "I promise I'll take such good care of him you won't even know he's around."

"Better not make promises you can't keep," Miss Arbutus said.

And that's how it happened that a three-legged dog became another permanent resident at The Roost.

8

M R. DOCTOR HAD CAUTIONED PETER NOT TO LET THE DOG attempt to walk more than was necessary for a while, to give the stump a chance to heal. So Ruby secured him in a cardboard box, which she lined with pieces of an old blanket. Then she placed the box beneath the window in her room and cared tenderly for the puppy. She carried him outside when she thought he needed to go, fed him leftovers from the table, gave him plenty of fresh water, and dosed him with crumbs of aspirin for his pain, as directed by Peter, who took his professional duties seriously.

When Ruby was in school, Grandma and Lucy Elkins were almost as attentive to the pup as Ruby was. Peter also kept his promise by researching fleas. He soon concocted a paste that he brought to Ruby.

"If you see even one flea, you have to spread this paste all over him," Peter directed. "Leave it on for an hour, then wash it off."

"Will do," Ruby agreed. "But what's in it?"

"My secret remedy," Peter said. "I can't disclose the ingredients. I may want to bottle it and sell it."

Peter also took some chicken wire and fashioned a sort of cage to fit in the back of Ruby's red Radio Flyer wagon, which she used for running errands. With the cage she could take the dog with her without worrying that he might fall out on the hard sidewalk. He could still see everything and greet the townspeople as they stopped to chat. In a matter of days everybody had become acquainted with him. Many people suggested names, but none of them seemed right to Ruby. So he was known only as Ruby's dog.

"I'll know the right name when it comes along," Ruby said.

One afternoon, while she was pulling her wagon to Morgan's Drugs to buy some things for Miss Arbutus, she saw her classmate Slim Morgan. He had his camera set up on a small platform with three poles holding it up.

"What'cha doin' there, Slim?" Ruby asked as she parked her wagon beside him.

Ruby's dog stood up and looked at Slim through the wire and wagged his tail. His eyes had become much brighter and his face happier as health had started to return. Slim poked his fingers through the wire and wiggled them.

"I'm taking a picture of the drugstore," he said as he stood erect and steadied his camera where it rested on the platform of the contraption.

"What for?"

"For *The Way Down Deep Daily*. Every Sunday they are going to feature one of the businesses in town—its history, its owners, and its services—and they need pictures. So that's what I'm doing."

"That's nice," Ruby said. "I guess they'll feature The Roost, too, won't they?"

"I'm sure they will," Slim said as he peeped through the window of his Hawkeye Brownie, which he had received as a present on his last birthday.

"Why have you got your camera sitting on top of that thing?" Ruby asked, pointing to the contraption. "Why don't you just hold it in your hand?"

"I saw a story in a magazine about a famous photographer, and there was a picture of him with his camera propped up on one of these," Slim said. "So I made me one, and when I become a photographer for *National Geographic*, I'll have some practice in using it. It's called a tripod because it has three legs."

"I didn't know you wanted to be a photographer," Ruby said.

"Yeah, I do. I like taking pictures better than anything. Daddy says I'm going to drive him to bankruptcy buying film for—"

"That's it!" Ruby interrupted him. "Tripod!"

"That's what?" Slim asked.

"My dog's name!" Ruby squealed. "Tripod! 'Cause he has only three legs."

"That's good," Slim said. "I like it."

Tripod wagged his tail and grinned. Yeah, he liked it, too.

* * *

On the fourth Saturday of October, Ruby, Peter, Cedar, and Tripod took the path up the mountain to see Granny Butler for the purpose of finding out something about Tripod's past. As they passed Jethro's grave, each of them stopped for a moment to pat the mound of earth and say hello. Ruby had not seen Jethro's shadow in quite some time, and she wondered if he had gone on to goat heaven or some such spiritual place. Or maybe he thought Ruby didn't need cheering up anymore since she got Tripod.

Taking turns carrying the dog, they hiked all the way to the mountaintop, where a giant tree sheltered Granny Butler's neat cabin.

As they approached, the thin, short woman came out the door and threw up a hand of greeting. Her milky white skin appeared almost translucent. Behind her wire-rimmed specs, the whites of her eyes had a pinkish hue, while the irises were a very light blue. This cool day she was wearing a blue cardigan sweater over her gingham house dress.

"There you are," she called. "I been expecting you."

Not only did Granny Butler have a way with animals, but she also had a knack for "seeing" when somebody was coming.

"Hey, Granny Butler," Ruby said. "Miss Arbutus and I want to thank you for the pumpkin. It's the biggest one I ever saw. We made a jack-o'-lantern for the front porch."

"What pumpkin?" Granny Butler said.

"That pumpkin on our porch didn't come from you?" Ruby said. "About two weeks back?"

"And how would I carry a big pumpkin all the way down this mountain to The Roost?" Granny Butler asked.

"Well, we thought maybe you got somebody to deliver it for you."

"Wasn't me, so you must have a secret admirer, Ruby," Granny Butler said with a chuckle, "which doesn't surprise me a bit, as pretty as you're turning out."

With Peter by her side, Ruby felt herself blushing at those words.

"And what's that you got there?" Granny Butler asked, squinting at Tripod.

Ruby turned to Peter. "Tell her the story."

"It was a trap," Granny Butler said, before Peter could speak.

Gently she took Tripod into her arms, and he gave her sloppy puppy kisses.

"What do you mean?" Peter asked.

"He was caught in a trap that was meant for a fox."

Ruby was horrified. "How awful!"

"But who would be mean enough to set a trap for a fox?" Peter wanted to know.

"Some chicken farmer, I reckon," Granny Butler said. "Foxes eat chickens, and men set traps for foxes. That's just the way of the world. But thank goodness it got only one leg." She set Tripod on her slate walkway. "Let's see how you walk without all your parts, little man."

Tripod limped toward Ruby for a dozen or so steps before

he fell. Granny Butler picked him up and cuddled him against her cheek.

"He's got a lot of heart," she said.

"We were hoping you could ask him about his past," Ruby said.

"Give me a minute," Granny Butler said. "Y'all stay where you're at."

Then she walked around the side of her cabin, mumbling to Tripod as she went. Tripod mumbled something in return as Ruby, Peter, and Cedar watched and waited patiently on the walkway.

"He's got amnesia," Granny Butler said when she returned after a few minutes.

Ruby started to laugh, then caught herself because the old woman's face was serious. "Amnesia?" she said.

"Yeah, he can't remember much about the trap, only that he was rescued by a big bald-headed man."

"And Tripod didn't know who he was?" Cedar spoke up.

Granny Butler looked Cedar up and down before answering him. "Boy, have you quit your cussin' ways since I saw you last summer?"

It was Cedar's turn to blush. He stuck both hands in his pockets and kicked a small stone off the walkway. "Yes, ma'am. I quit cussin' a while back, 'cept for once when I messed up."

"How can he have amnesia?" Peter came back to the subject. "I never knew dogs had much of a memory to start with."

"This little feller knows y'all, don't he?" Granny Butler said. "That's 'cause he remembers you from day to day."

"How did he get to our yard?" Cedar asked.

"Baldy took him there. That was the man's name. He found Tripod in the trap, got him out, and took him to your house 'cause he knew you'd take care of him."

And Granny Butler could tell them no more.

"He's still a pup," she explained, "and he can't express himself like a big dog can."

So now they knew what had happened to Tripod's leg, and they knew that a big man had rescued him. But who was that man? Who was Baldy?

9

HALLOWEEN PRANKS AND TRICK OR TREAT WERE TWO DIFFER-
ent customs in Way Down. Soaping screens was the
worst Halloween prank ever to be pulled in that town. It was
done by taking a bar of soap and grinding it into the screen on
somebody's window. A person could never get the scum out of
a screen that had been soaped. Adults had rated that prank
high on the disapproval scale, so it had long ago been discon-
tinued. Ruby and her classmates heard of it only from previous
generations.

There was also a legend that some hillbilly boys—obviously
without a lick of sense—had rolled a log across Highway 99
one dark Halloween night, causing more grief than they had
bargained for, but anything that god-awful was beyond the
imaginations of the youngsters of Way Down. Their only aim
was to have fun, not to hurt anybody. It was also understood
that you couldn't take Halloween pranks personally. Learning
to laugh at yourself helped build character.

The most common prank these days was the dollar-on-the-sidewalk one. That's where you put a thread through the corner of a dollar bill, and laid it on the sidewalk, then hid close by where you could watch. Without fail, some yokel came along and reached for it, and you jerked it away by the thread.

Another one was pouring bubble bath into the toilet tanks at school. Or you could hoist a pair of flashy drawers up the flagpole in front of the courthouse and send out the rumor that they belonged to some prominent person—like the mayor or the Presbyterian minister; it didn't have to be true. Or you could send something perishable to somebody through the mail. A couple of raw eggs would do, but a fish was even better. That was the reason Mrs. Farmer, the postmistress, wore rubber gloves when she handled the mail around Halloween.

Every year the kids would lie awake nights trying to come up with an original prank. Sometimes they succeeded but usually not. In that case they fell back on the old tried-and-true ones.

As for trick or treat, it worked in Way Down as in most other places. The kids almost always got their sweets. If somebody failed to treat them, which was rare, they did nothing but move to the next house. They consistently went home happy with a bag full of candy, and to bed with a bellyache.

Halloween was to fall on Sunday that year of 1954, so the kids were planning to trick-or-treat on Saturday night. On the Thursday before, Miss Duke's second-period English class was busy making up compound sentences to diagram, while she was reading their quarterly book reports, which they had turned in earlier.

"Johnny Ray Springstep!" Miss Duke yelled suddenly. "Stop talking."

Once again Johnny Ray was caught red-handed and red-faced.

"I was helping Reese with his diagramming," Johnny Ray tried to explain.

"If Reese needs help, he can come to me," Miss Duke said.

Reese at that moment was like the deer in the headlights. Ask Miss Duke for help? Nothin' doin'. He'd rather flunk English.

"So what's your problem?" Miss Duke prodded Reese.

"It's a sentence about Halloween," Reese mumbled. "But you know what, Miss Duke? I think I got it now. Never mind."

"Halloween! Huh!" Miss Duke snorted. "I'd rather you didn't use a sentence about Halloween. It's the stupidest holiday ever invented."

"Yes, ma'am," Reese said agreeably. "I'll change it to something else."

Immediately every pencil eraser in the room went into action rubbing out all references to Halloween. But Miss Duke was not finished.

"And let me give all of you fair warning," she went on. "Don't come knocking at my door begging for candy."

The kids just stared at her without speaking their minds, which was probably best. Still, she read something in their dark expressions and simply had to address it. How could she not?

"So you think I'm mean, do you?" she said to them. "Well, I'll tell you what's mean. Using a fake holiday to extort candy out of a person, now *that's* mean."

It crossed the mind of more than one kid in the room that she sounded exactly like Scrooge commenting on Christmas. How did people get to be like that?

Johnny Ray spoke up again. "Don't worry, Miss Duke. I'm pretty sure that nobody is going to bother you on Halloween night."

"And how do you know that, Johnny Ray?"

It was on the tip of Johnny Ray's tongue to say, "Because we've got other witches to deal with on that night."

But just in the nick of time he heard a voice in his head that sounded exactly like Mr. Bear's. "Be nice to Miss Duke, Johnny Ray, and I'll tutor you privately in chemistry during your study hall."

No, he wouldn't disappoint Mr. Bear, and he wouldn't give up his chemistry lessons.

"Because we wouldn't want to trouble you, ma'am," he said to Miss Duke instead.

Then Johnny Ray flashed an ear-to-ear smile that unnerved the teacher. She couldn't help wondering why he had been so nice to her lately. Did he have some trick up his sleeve?

The break bell rang, and the students fled Miss Duke's class. On that day Johnny Ray, Reese, and Cedar leaned against the fence in the last warm glow of autumn and talked together while they watched a hot game of marbles between two other boys. Cedar, who was in the seventh grade and would suffer through

Miss Duke's English class later that day, had not yet heard the Halloween lecture, so Johnny Ray and Reese summarized it for him in advance.

Cedar rolled his eyes, sighed glumly, and said, "I learned something interesting from Ruby's grandma the other day. Did you know that when you want to hire somebody for a job, you can put an ad in the newspaper? Wouldn't it be nice if we could pick our teachers that way?"

"Yeah," Reese said. "Then we could replace Miss Duke."

"Not a bad idea!" Johnny Ray said.

"Whaddaya mean?" Cedar said.

"Why not do that for a Halloween prank?" Johnny Ray said. "Run an ad for Miss Duke's job? Don't you think it would be funny?"

"It would make *me* laugh," Reese said.

"It would make everybody laugh," Johnny Ray said.

"Any ad, any length, twenty-five cents," Cedar said. "That's what it says on the top of the page where the ads are."

"We could raise twenty-five cents," Johnny Ray said. "Here, I'll put in the first nickel."

He reached into his pants pocket, pulled out the only coin he had to his name, and held it in the palm of his hand.

"Here's my nickel," Cedar said, and added his money to Johnny Ray's.

"And here's mine," Reese said, tossing in the third coin.

"I'll betcha we can get a nickel from Slim," Johnny Ray said.

"I'm sure we can."

So they called Slim over and explained what they were doing. Slim laughed, then reached into his pocket and pulled out a quarter. "Give me your three nickels, and I'll put in my case quarter," he said.

"Done!"

The next morning during break, Johnny Ray, Reese, Slim, and Cedar, with their heads together, chuckled as they looked over the ad Johnny Ray had written in large block letters so that nobody would recognize his handwriting. Then the boys took the quarter and taped it to the ad.

"I'll get an envelope from Mama's desk this evening," Reese volunteered, "and I'll put the ad in the envelope and take it to the newspaper down in the basement of the library. They have a slot in the door there for people to slip in stuff they want to go in the paper."

"It's the best Halloween prank ever!" Slim declared.

It so happened that, only the week before, the newspaper had filled the position of typesetter apprentice with an eager but green eighteen-year-old named Jude. Being inexperienced, Jude did not know what the seasoned employees knew—that the school board would never hire a teacher through a common help wanted ad. They always turned to professional publications for that purpose.

Therefore, when the prank ad fell into Jude's hands that Friday evening, he didn't think of questioning its authenticity. Instead, he decided to practice what he had been learning. He typeset the words without help from anybody. When the ad appeared in black-and-white on Saturday morning in *The Way Down Deep Daily*, Jude couldn't have been more pleased with his handiwork.

HELP WANTED: PRONTO.
ENGLISH TEACHER FOR 7TH AND
8TH GRADE AT WDD SCHOOL.
MUST NOT BE A GRUMPY OLD GROUCH.
CALL OLIVE 4010.

10

WHEN THE TOWNSPEOPLE READ THE BOGUS AD ON SATUR-day, most of them recognized it as a Halloween prank, and quite a good one at that. Even the high school boys were impressed, and wondered what genius had dreamed it up. It had to be somebody in one of Miss Duke's classes. Nobody knew anything for sure except the boys involved, and they weren't talking.

Upon finding out that he had unwittingly taken part in a prank, Jude, the new typesetter, figured he was going to be in deep trouble—just as soon as his supervisor stopped laughing.

And what about Miss Duke? Being an educator, she always read the newspaper from cover to cover, every word of it, and that day was no exception. Not having grown up in Way Down, she didn't quite get it that she shouldn't take the prank person-ally. After reading the ad, she sat in her small apartment and stared for a long, long time at a photograph hanging on the wall. It was the likeness of a woman wearing a sad housedress, her hair pulled back into an old-fashioned bun, her hands twisted around each other, her eyes empty and unfocused. Miss Duke was still sitting there when darkness fell, but she didn't bother to turn on a light.

Ruby did not go trick-or-treating anymore. She got a bigger kick out of giving away candy to the other kids. So that night— with a dilapidated broom, a long rubber nose with a bump on it, and a pointed black hat made of construction paper—she dressed as a witch and stayed in the common room at The Roost all evening to answer the door and hand out candy. She allowed Tripod to explore only if he agreed not to get out of her sight, and he promised. The stump of his missing leg had healed nicely, and he was getting around fairly well on his three good legs.

Only the Way Down kids came to her door, as the out-of-towners had trick or treat in their own neighborhoods. At nine o'clock, the small clusters of revelers had stopped, so Ruby took Tripod out for his last break, then outed the candle in the jack-o'-lantern on the porch, and went for her evening visit with Miss Arbutus.

The two of them were happily chatting, when Miss Arbutus suddenly glanced toward the window with an anxious expression on her face. In the next moment Miss Arbutus stood up and briskly left the room. Ruby followed her with Tripod close behind. They found Miss Arbutus standing on the porch at the top of the steps trying to look at her surroundings, but the night was as black as ink. She cocked her head to one side as if listening, then sniffed the air. Ruby slipped a hand into Miss Arbutus's hand.

"What is it?" she whispered.

"It's an evil wind, Ruby. An evil wind blowing into our little town."

Ruby whispered again. "Evil? What do you mean?"

"I can smell it and I can feel it. My mother used to tell me stories of evil winds bringing bad tidings."

"Bad tidings in Way Down? How can that be?"

"I don't know, dear."

Ruby twined one arm around Miss Arbutus's thin waist, and they stood there together for a moment shivering in the cold breeze. Yes, it did have an unusual feel, Ruby thought. Tripod rubbed against her leg, asking to be included in the hug. So she reached down and picked him up.

In her cold, dark apartment, Miss Duke had forgotten to eat supper, and trick-or-treaters had not disturbed her. Without undressing, she had gone to bed late but did not sleep. She lay staring at the window until the sun came up. It was the last day of October, her birthday, but nobody in the world besides her knew or cared.

When Ruby woke up on Sunday morning, she dressed and carried Tripod outside. She fed him on the back porch, then left him there to play while she ate breakfast. He was learning to get up and down the porch steps by himself, and he liked to play in the fenced part of the yard.

At breakfast Mr. Crawford gave them some bad news that was on the front page of *The Way Down Deep Daily*. One hundred men were to be laid off at the Cold Branch Mine.

"Bad news for this whole area," Lucy said. "Way Down will certainly feel the pinch."

Ruby's and Miss Arbutus's eyes met across the table. Could this be the work of the evil wind?

At school on Monday morning all the chatter was of the prank ad—that is, until they got to Miss Duke's class. Then the smiles were wiped away and every child was as serious as a parson. Although everybody thought the prank was funny, nobody wanted to be suspected by Miss Duke of being the mastermind. So they put on their innocent faces.

Though Miss Duke looked as drab that day as she had on Friday, there was something different about her face. All the kids noticed it, but nobody could put a finger on what the difference was. Of course, if she had given them a big smile, now *that* would certainly have been a change. She didn't do that, but she didn't frown either. She didn't sneer or make sarcastic remarks. She didn't even holler at anybody. She was just very, very quiet. And that made her students very, very nervous. In fact, they moved around as if on thin ice.

When the break bell rang, the middle grades tumbled out into the November day and Miss Duke found herself alone with her thoughts in the empty classroom. She remained at her desk and, for no reason at all, thought of Ruby. It seemed that everybody gravitated toward the girl, even the adults. She had more friends than anybody else did.

Miss Duke pushed a strand of hair out of her face, looked toward the school yard, and allowed memories to engulf her. She didn't remember her dad, and her mom had had to work all the time. Miss Duke's mom hadn't had time for friends, nor did she have time for her only child. So the child had raised herself. At her mom's funeral last year, Miss Duke had been the only one in attendance. Would that be her own fate someday?

Once she had dreamed of getting married and having a family of her own, but young men had never shown any interest in her.

She had been aware that her students called her a mean old grump even before she had read the unflattering prank ad, but wasn't it her job to teach them, not to be friends with them?

The last semester before she graduated, a helpful college professor had warned Miss Duke that she would have to learn how to bend in the classroom so that she wouldn't break. At the time she had been puzzled by the professor's remark. Now she understood, because she was on the verge of breaking. She could not continue being the same person. But she was afraid she did not have the courage to change.

She placed her head upon her arms across her desk and began to cry. Had Ruby witnessed this incident she might have thought this woman didn't even resemble that overbearing teacher who caused nightmares in children. She was simply a sad person.

The bell rang, and Miss Duke hurriedly blotted her eyes dry. No matter how heavy her heart, she would have to hide her tears from the kids and somehow get through this day.

That same afternoon, as Miss Duke was leaving the school grounds, her old dilapidated car sputtered and finally died. She had known for some time that it was on its way out, but today it seemed like the last straw. She was afraid she might cry again, right here in a public place. She would have to ask somebody for help, a thing she was always loath to do.

Fortunately for Miss Duke, Ruby happened to be playing with Tripod in front of The Roost that afternoon, and it was she who noticed Miss Duke's dilemma. To ignore a person in need was not in Ruby's nature, even if that person was Miss Duke. She left Tripod on the porch with Grandma and skipped across the street to where the teacher sat in her useless car, trying to decide what to do.

"Hey, Miss Duke, need some help?" Ruby asked pleasantly.

Miss Duke looked out at Ruby through the open window of her car. "Oh, it's you."

"Yes, ma'am. Looks like you're having car trouble. Want me to call a mechanic for you?"

"The junkyard's more like it," Miss Duke said. "I think this old heap is good for nothing else now."

"Oh," Ruby said, because she didn't know what else to say.

Miss Duke was at a loss as well. Even if she could get a ride home, how would she get back to school tomorrow? Most people in Way Down would simply call around and find somebody who was going the same way, but that solution did not occur to Miss Duke because she knew nobody to call.

"It would be lots easier for you if you lived at The Roost," Ruby commented, then immediately bit her tongue.

But she was too late. To her horror Miss Duke looked in the direction of The Roost, nodded her head, and said, "Yes, Ruby. You're right. If I lived here, I wouldn't need a car at all."

Ruby was speechless. What had she done?

"Is there a room available now?" Miss Duke asked her.

Ruby simply bobbed her head up and down, because she couldn't bring herself to say out loud to Miss Duke that there was indeed an empty room on the second floor diagonally across from her own spacious pastel boudoir.

Miss Duke gave Ruby something that might pass for a ghost of a smile, and said, "Then I think the simplest thing for me to do is to find someone who will help me move tonight."

11

MISS ARBUTUS ARRANGED FOR JUNIOR MULLINS, THE OLD-est of the Mullins children, to use his daddy's pickup truck, fetch Miss Duke, and help her pack and move some of her belongings to The Roost that evening. She also called Tony Leghorn at the Shimpock junkyard and arranged to have the Buick towed away. When Miss Duke arrived at The Roost, all the other residents were having a lively discussion over supper and didn't pay attention when Miss Arbutus and Ruby left the table to help the teacher carry her few boxes to her room on the second floor. As they went up the stairs raucous laughter spilled out from the dining room.

"Supper is on the table," Miss Arbutus said. "So why don't you come on down and let me introduce you to the other boarders. You must be starving."

The very idea of sitting around a table—eating and making conversation with strangers—struck dread in Miss Duke's heart.

"Oh, no, I'm not hungry at all," she said.

"But you must eat," Miss Arbutus insisted.

"I have a few snacks," Miss Duke explained. "It's all I will need tonight."

"You're sure?"

"Quite sure."

"All right, then. Come, Ruby, let's give Miss Duke some privacy," Miss Arbutus said kindly, and the two of them left.

The teacher collapsed onto the bed, listening to the sounds in the large house. She heard doors opening and closing, and friendly voices talking and laughing. So dinner was probably over, she was thinking, and now the residents were involved in private pursuits for the evening. She knew she would be reading for a couple of hours before sleeping. It's what she had been in the habit of doing since childhood. She wondered if these other people would be doing things together.

At last she rose up from her bed and put away some of the items she had brought with her. She had left half of her belongings in the garage apartment, mostly books packed in boxes, but Junior Mullins had promised to go for them tomorrow while she was at work.

She took a moment then to look around the room. It was nice—fairly large, clean, well furnished, and simply but tastefully decorated. She examined the closet and drawer space. Quite adequate. She walked to the window and looked out. Her room faced the street, and though it was dark by this time, she could see the outline of the school directly in front of her. Yes, very convenient.

At that moment she noticed a tall man walking on the sidewalk. Just as he went under a streetlight, he pulled his jacket tight across his chest, then turned his face to the sky as if looking for signs of weather. She could not help noticing what a nice strong face he had. When the man reached The Roost walkway, he turned onto it. She could hear the door downstairs opening and closing as he entered the common room. So he must be staying here. Temporarily, she wondered, or permanently?

Then someone knocked on her door and she nearly jumped out of her skin. It was Lucy Elkins, here to introduce herself and welcome the newcomer. Lucy was the kind of gentle lady who always tried to see the nice things about a person, and that night her first impression of Miss Duke was that she had very pretty eyes, even though they were filled with sadness.

"I'm sure Miss Arbutus pointed out the bathroom to you there at the end of the hall," Lucy said brightly.

Miss Duke nodded but said nothing.

"All right, then," Lucy said. "If you need anything, I'm right next door."

When Lucy opened the door to leave, Miss Duke could see Ruby playing with her three-legged dog in the hallway. She waited until Lucy had gone into her room and closed the door before going out to take a closer look.

"This is Tripod," Ruby said.

Instantly Miss Duke's face relaxed. She went down on her knees in front of Tripod, and actually gathered him into her arms. "What happened to his leg?"

Ruby sat down on the floor beside Miss Duke. "He was caught in a trap."

"A trap?" Miss Duke said as she cuddled Tripod to her. "Oh yes, Tripod, I know about traps."

Tripod licked her face happily as if he were greeting an old friend after a long separation, and for the first time in a long time Miss Duke actually smiled.

Encouraged, Ruby said, "He just loves people, and everybody at The Roost loves him back."

"How many people live here all the time?" Miss Duke asked.

Ruby started counting on her fingers. "There's me and Rita and you and Miss Arbutus and Grandma and Lucy and Mr. Crawford. That's seven."

"Who is Mr. Crawford?" Miss Duke asked.

"He's a writer. He's writing a book about Way Down. He's the only man right now, so he's got the third floor all to himself."

Miss Duke found this bit of information interesting. Maybe the people in this town were not *all* backward. Suddenly she found that her heart was beating faster.

"I see," she managed to say very calmly, "and your grandma lives here, too?"

"Yes, ma'am. She lives right there beside my room. She used to be mad at the world, but now she's not anymore."

That was a strange comment, Miss Duke was thinking. Mad at the world?

"And Lucy was a real debutante," Ruby said. "All the women in her family married into high society and became elegant ladies. But Lucy fell in love with a sawmill worker and married him instead of a rich man, and her family disowned her. Don't you think that was mean of them?"

Miss Duke nodded her head. Tripod seemed to be going to sleep against her knees as she petted him.

"Then when her husband died," Ruby went on, "Lucy had no place to go. She came to The Roost to recuperate for a while, and that turned into forever. When she ran out of money, Miss Arbutus didn't have the heart to turn her out, so—"

Ruby suddenly clasped both hands over her mouth. She had said too much. Miss Arbutus never brought up the fact that Lucy was unable to pay her rent, and she would not allow anybody else to mention it either.

"Oh, forget I said that part," Ruby pleaded. "Please? I talk too much."

Miss Duke nodded her head again. She was thinking how bad Lucy must feel being a dependent in the prime of her life. Perhaps she could be friends with Lucy Elkins.

"And Rita is Peter and Cedar Reeder's little sister. She lives here during the school week. Her mommie died last year, so Miss Arbutus became her substitute mommie. Rita's a sweetheart."

When bedtime came, Miss Duke found she was too wound up to sleep or even to read. The vague sound of Mr. Crawford's typewriter came to her as she lay awake, thinking about how awful her day had started out, but maybe The Roost was just the thing she needed. She knew it wouldn't be easy to change. Then after promising herself that nobody would ever again have a reason to call her a grumpy grouch, she fell into a deep dreamless sleep.

12

WHEN MISS DUKE APPEARED AT BREAKFAST THE NEXT morning, all the boarders greeted her warmly and welcomed her to The Roost. She gave them a tentative smile and settled down to eat with them. She did not feel comfortable entering the conversation right away, so she sat quietly as she ate and listened and learned.

Miss Duke's students noticed her entering and leaving The Roost instead of driving the Buick to school, and they figured out the obvious. She had moved in. They felt sorry for poor Ruby, having to live under the same roof with the grumpy grouch, having to share meals with her, and never being able to get away from her.

"It's not so bad," Ruby told her classmates when they asked her about it. "We don't see much of her." And she would say no more, regardless of relentless questioning.

Soon the kids and other teachers began to detect a change in Miss Duke's behavior. She remained unusually subdued in the classroom, and never lost her temper anymore. She smiled a nervous smile once in a while. As time went by, she even began to take on a different appearance. She came to school wearing the same clothes she had worn before, but now they seemed to fit her better and be more fashionable. The kids noticed that those green cat-eye reading glasses, which had always made Miss Duke look meaner, now actually brought out the color of her eyes and made her look more girlish.

One day when she caught Johnny Ray talking during silent reading time, Miss Duke walked calmly to his desk and whispered to him, "Could you please hold it down while others are trying to concentrate?"

Johnny Ray was more startled by the teacher's whispering than by her yelling. Not only was she speaking softly, but when she bent over his desk, she threw off a pleasant aroma, like oranges or lemons. He nodded his head in response, for he was speechless, and that was a condition he was not familiar with.

One evening Miss Duke looked at the stark black-and-white photo of the woman in the sad housedress and the granny hairdo, which was now hanging on the wall of her new room. She wondered how old her mother was when that picture was taken. She must still have been young, so why did she look like a . . . ? A what? A grumpy old grouch!

Ruby, Lucy, Rita, and Tripod visited Miss Duke in her room and felt welcome. Miss Arbutus did not visit, but she made a point of speaking to Miss Duke every time she saw her. Chit-chat did not come naturally to either one of them, but Miss Duke found it became easier with practice. On a Saturday afternoon when all the other residents were busy elsewhere, she decided it was time to get to know Ruby's grandma. Quietly, she went out and sat down beside her in one of the white rocking chairs on the porch.

Grandma, of course, was always eager and ready to have a friendly conversation with anybody these days, and she began straightaway telling Miss Duke the story of her life and what had brought her to The Roost.

"I was so dadblamed mean, my other grandchildren, my son's three boys, wouldn't even come to see me," Grandma said. "Then Ruby came for a visit. It's a wonder she didn't leave that first day, but she stayed for most of the summer, and I'm certainly glad she didn't give up on me."

Miss Duke cringed because she saw herself in Grandma's self-portrait. She had been such a mean old teacher that the kids had wanted to replace her. When Grandma told her about Ruby's magical trip to Way Down, she didn't scoff in the least and say it was a tall tale, as she would have done not too long ago. Now she was hoping to get a little of that magic for herself.

"Miss Arbutus is a mystic, isn't she?" she whispered.

Grandma didn't really know the meaning of that word, but she could guess. She replied, "Yeah, she's one of them—what you said."

"And Ruby is a special child?"

Grandma agreed. "Absolutely. Just a little girl, and she fussed at me for being so whiny. She made me see I had to put aside whatever had happened to me in the past and take responsibility for myself."

Miss Duke said, "I've never had a friend before, and I feel very lucky to have those two."

"You also have me and Lucy," Grandma reminded her.

"Of course!" Miss Duke agreed. "And sweet little Rita, and Tripod, too. He's my buddy."

Ruby had been leaving Tripod in Miss Duke's room in the evening when she went for private time with Miss Arbutus and Rita. Having never had a pet in her life, Miss Duke had not realized how much she was in need of one. Now she found she could hardly wait to share her thoughts and feelings with the little dog at the end of the day. Tripod was a good listener, and never scolded or judged her. He was also a clown, and made her laugh out loud as she remembered doing when she was a very small girl.

For Thanksgiving dinner Miss Duke dressed in a plaid wool skirt with a dark green pullover sweater. It was what all the college girls were wearing last winter. She looked at herself in the mirror. She had never before noticed how shiny her chestnut hair was, and how it curled softly around her oval face. She liked what she saw, for it was like looking at somebody young and pleasant.

She looked at the photo on the wall. "I look nice, Mom," she said, "because I'm learning to *be* nice."

She headed for the dining room. When she walked in slightly late, the other guests were already seated at the table. Mr. Crawford was standing with a carving knife in one hand, ready to do the honors. Miss Duke hesitated in the doorway for a few seconds, and all eyes went to her. A chorus of warm compliments followed.

"How nice you look."

"What a sweet outfit."

"And your hair is lovely."

She flashed a brilliant smile, walked to the table, and sat down at the empty place beside Ruby. Her face was as pink as a rose, and her eyes sparkled in the light.

Mr. Crawford stood still, knife poised but motionless as he stared at her. Was this the same plain, timid creature he had been dining with daily for the last three weeks? Had he actually bothered to look at her before? Perhaps he should pay more attention.

He lowered the knife to the table and said to his fellow diners, "Our newest guest should have the choicest cut of the turkey, don't you agree?"

"Yes, of course."

"By all means."

Mr. Crawford smiled at Miss Duke. "And which cut would you prefer, my lady?"

Miss Duke and Mr. Crawford began spending evenings in the common room, playing rummy with anybody who would take them on. Although card games were new to Miss Duke, Mr. Crawford seemed delighted to coach her. They would set up their card table in a corner as far from the radio as possible, so as not to disturb the listeners.

The week after Thanksgiving Judge Elbert Deel joined

them. He had come to town to hold court. He presided over a full roster of cases during the week and still would not be finished until the middle of the following week, so he relished these moments of relaxation with the other guests at The Roost. His partner was Lucy, who had been competing in different games with the guests for so long that she had become something of an expert. Most people were reluctant to play against her.

This week also brought more bad news to the coal mining communities. Additional layoffs were announced, and some of the smaller mines closed altogether. Miss Arbutus told Ruby and Rita that she could feel the evil wind almost daily now, and it warned her to be prepared for hard times.

On Sunday morning it was in the paper that the Black Snake Mine was closing, forcing seventy men out of work indefinitely. At school on Monday Ruby noticed that Johnny Ray and the other kids from Black Snake Holler were not themselves. They did their work, responded when spoken to, ate their baloney sandwiches, and did all the other usual things, but they were obviously worried. Ruby knew, as all West Virginians did, that the mining families were too proud for their own good. Even in dire circumstances they would stick together and never grumble to outsiders.

That night Ruby stood brushing Miss Arbutus's long dark hair before the mirror.

"What will they do?" she asked.

"They lived off the land for two hundred years as hunters and farmers," Miss Arbutus said, "and some of them still do.

But most of them are used to wages now, and it will be difficult for them to lose that steady income. They will do the best they can. They will survive for a while on whatever meager savings they have managed to put away, and rely on one another."

The following week two more mines closed down.

"It seems they could have waited until after Christmas," Ruby said to Miss Arbutus.

"I'm sure they stayed open as long as they could," Miss Arbutus said. "But they can't mine coal if it's no longer there."

"What about more mines opening?" Ruby asked. "Aren't they always looking for new seams of coal?"

"Yes," Miss Arbutus said. "But there's no guarantee they will find them."

13

On the Saturday morning before Christmas, Ruby dressed in her winter gear and, carrying a hatchet, went knocking on the Reeders' front door. Tripod was with her. Peter answered the knock.

"You wanna help me find a Christmas tree for The Roost?" she asked him.

"Sure. Let me get my jacket," Peter said.

"You gonna leave me here to look after Bird?" Cedar said a bit crossly.

Bird was Robber Bob's father, and grandfather to the five Reeder children. He was way over sixty, but Peter had once told Ruby that Bird was going through his second childhood. Sometimes he didn't know what year it was, or even where he was. Sometimes he babbled nonsense and at other times he was as lucid as anybody. When Robber Bob was working, Peter and Cedar were expected to look after their grandfather.

"We can take him with us," Ruby said.

"You sure?" Peter said. "He can get on your nerves pretty bad."

"The fresh air will do him good," Ruby said.

Rita popped her head around the edge of the door. "Can I come, too?"

"Us too! Us too!" Skeeter and Jeeter chimed in.

"Why not?" Ruby said with a laugh. "Bring the whole family."

"We can get ourselves a tree, too, while we're at it," Cedar said.

"Okay, Bird, go get your teeth," Peter reminded the old man. "You forgot to put 'em in this morning, didn't you?"

When all jackets, hats, gloves, and teeth were in place, Ruby cried, "Then let's get on with it! Forward march!"

Peter and Ruby led the way with Tripod, while Cedar and Rita followed close behind. Skeeter and Jeeter brought up the rear with Bird between them to keep him from straying.

They didn't take the route of Way Up That-a-Way, but instead climbed a different hill where you could see a patch of evergreens from town. There was no path here to guide them as they hiked into the woods. Ruby was glad to escape momentarily from her worries over the mining families and enjoy the day with Peter and his family.

As Peter stopped to clip a bough of holly, Rita sidled up to Ruby and took her hand. "Did you get a ribbon for the button?"

Ruby was puzzled. "What?"

"The present I gave you for your birthday. Did you get a ribbon for it?"

Ruby was mortified. She had forgotten all about Rita's present and didn't even know where it was. She couldn't let Rita know that. It would really hurt her feelings. Of the many times they had been together since Ruby's birthday, she was surprised that Rita hadn't thought to bring up the subject before now.

"No, I haven't found the right ribbon yet, Rita, but I will. I think I should get a blue one, don't you?"

Her mind was racing. What had she done with that button?

"I reckon Santa Claus might bring you a blue ribbon," Rita said.

Ruby squeezed the little girl's hand. "That would be peachy."

At that moment Tripod, with ears laid back in the breeze and grinning all over, came tearing through the woods, chased by the twins. He had become so nimble on his three legs he could outrun them easily.

"Old Red!" Bird called out suddenly and grabbed for Tripod, but the speed demon was too quick for him, too.

Peter came up beside his grandfather and patted him on the back. "It's not Old Red, Bird. This dog doesn't even look like him."

Ruby knew that Old Red had been Bird's dog when he was a kid. These days he mistook every dog he saw for the dog of his childhood.

"Come 'ere, boy!" Bird called in his thin, creaky voice. "Come to me!"

They entered the patch of evergreens, and a cold white sun filtered through the branches onto the ground littered with pine needles and cones. Ruby breathed in the aroma of pine and cedar, which was always a reminder of happy Christmases past.

"Smell it?" she said to Peter.

"Yeah," Peter replied. "Peppermint and spicy apple cider."

Ruby smiled. "And cinnamon sticks and wood smoke curling from the chimney into the sky."

It would be nice if, when she grew old and addled like Bird, she could still remember things like these. She wouldn't mind forgetting how to conjugate a verb or what cod liver oil tasted like. Ah, but the smells of Christmas and the feeling of crisp December days like this one were welcome to stay in some obscure wrinkle of her brain forever.

Rita interrupted the moment with a shout. "I want this one!" And they turned to the task at hand.

Half an hour later they were all happy with the trees they had chosen. A medium-sized one would go to the Reeders, and a gigantic one to The Roost. With gloves to protect their fingers from the prickly spines, they took turns dragging the trees down the hillside into the valley.

"You can help, too," Ruby said to Bird, and he grinned like a kid tickled to be doing a grown-up job.

They dumped the Reeders' tree on their porch, to be dealt with later, before going to The Roost with the larger one. In the common room Miss Arbutus had brought out all the tree trimmings that had been accumulating over the years. The Reeders were fascinated with real store-bought decorations—strings of lights, garlands, icicles, snowflakes, a star for the top. There were glass ornaments of every color, with dates printed on them in red, going all the way back to 1891. Some years were missing.

"They get broken, you know," Ruby explained. "We used to have some from the 1880s, but they're no longer with us."

"These dagnab lights are all tangled up in knots," Cedar said.

So they spent the first twenty minutes untangling the light cords. About the time they were finished, Mr. Crawford came in from an invigorating walk with Miss Duke. Her cheeks were like apples. When they asked if they could help trim the tree, Peter and Cedar suddenly went bashful and stood aside, wondering if Miss Duke would spoil their afternoon.

"Sure you can help," Ruby said. "You're just in time to stand it up."

Mr. Crawford propped the tree into its container while Miss Arbutus and Miss Duke tightened the screws into the base. Peter and Cedar watched their teacher closely. Yeah, she was acting like a normal person.

"Pretty lady," Bird said suddenly, and pointed at Miss Duke.

She was so pleased she didn't know where to look. She stole a peek at Mr. Crawford, who smiled at her.

She smiled also, then said to Bird, "Thank you kindly, sir."

It was the incident that broke the last sliver of ice, and Peter and Cedar were back in the spirit of things. Throughout that memorable afternoon they laughed and joked with their teacher, and even sang a couple of carols as they strung the lights and garlands and hung the bulbs. Then Ruby asked Skeeter, Jeeter, and Rita to toss the icicles and snowflakes.

"Can't wait to tell Johnny Ray about this," Peter whispered to Cedar. "He's not gonna believe it."

"About what? Decorating a Christmas tree?" Cedar said.

"No, decorating it with you-know-who."

When all the pretty things were on the tree, Miss Arbutus brought out her new ornament for the year. It was a blue glass ball trimmed in silver.

"Ruby, will you do the honors?" she said.

With a tiny brush and red paint supplied by Miss Arbutus, Ruby painted *1954* on the bottom of the bulb. She retraced the date several times so that it would last at least fifty years. *Another Christmas memory to hold in my heart forever,* she thought as she hung the ball on the tree and her friends clapped their hands.

When the Reeders were on their way out the door at suppertime, Miss Arbutus called to them, "Tell Mr. Reeder that we would be pleased to have you all for Christmas dinner."

It was the perfect ending to the perfect day.

14

THAT NIGHT RUBY SEARCHED HER BRAIN AND HER ROOM FOR the button that Rita had given her. Through her jewelry box, her bureau and dresser drawers, her keepsake box. What was she thinking to let it get away from her? Well, she was probably thinking of Jethro. After all, her birthday was the day he died. She had been distracted. But what would she have done with it?

Her closet was the last place left to look. A coat pocket maybe? No, it was still warm weather on her birthday. What was she wearing? The gold dress! And it all came back to her. She found the dress and slipped a hand into the small pocket. Yes, there it was—a pewter-colored metal button. She clutched it to her heart, then took it to the lamp and held it close to the light. There was the hole someone had drilled into it, and around the hole were foreign words and strange symbols that she had not noticed when she first saw it.

The next evening when Rita came back to The Roost, Ruby asked her, "Where did you get this button?"

"A man gave it to me."

"What man?"

"I was in the yard catching lightning bugs, and a man came by," Rita said.

"Who was he?"

"I don't know."

"It was dark, and you weren't afraid of him?" Ruby asked.

"No, he twinkled, and he was funny." Rita giggled.

"He twinkled?"

"Yeah. He twinkled blue all over."

He twinkled blue?

"After he gave you the button, what happened?"

"Nothing," Rita said.

"Did the man leave then?"

"Yeah, he left."

"Have you seen him again since then?"

"Nope."

"Did anybody else see him? Your daddy maybe, or Peter?"

"No. They were all in the house canning blackberries."

"Oh, it was blackberry season," Ruby said. "Who put the hole in the button?"

"That man said he did it for you," Rita said.

Ruby was taken aback. "For me? The man said the button was for me?"

"Yeah, he said it was to go on a ribbon for Ruby."

"I was on Yonder Mountain during blackberry season," Ruby said.

"Yeah," Rita said. "But the man said you'd be coming back."

How could a stranger have known a thing like that?

When all thirteen guests were seated around the table for Christmas dinner at The Roost, they joined hands and recited the "Prayer Perfect" together:

> *"Bring unto the sorrowing all release from pain;*
> *Let the lips of laughter overflow again,*
> *And for all the needy, oh, divide, I pray,*
> *This vast treasure of content that is mine today."*

When the food was passed around, Mr. Crawford, sitting beside Miss Duke, made the announcement that his long-awaited book was finished and that he would be dropping it in the mail come Monday morning. A chorus of cheers followed, for it was hard to believe that he had actually finished writing *A Colorful History of Way Down Deep, West Virginia.*

"For a few years now I've been in touch with an editor at a publishing house in New York City who wants to publish it," Mr. Crawford told them. "He's anxious to see the completed manuscript."

"And when can we expect to have a signed copy for The Roost?" Ruby asked.

"Perhaps this time next year."

Everybody groaned. "Next year?"

"Maybe two years," Mr. Crawford said. "There are many stages in turning a manuscript into a real book. It takes time."

Both turkey and ham were on the table, along with biscuits and gravy, potatoes, several kinds of vegetables, and salads. Rita, of course, had become accustomed to eating at The Roost, but Robber Bob, Bird, and the boys had not had such a feast as this in a long time. They relished every bite. In fact, everybody at the table ate until they were as stuffed as the turkey itself, chatting all the while and enjoying this special celebration in the company of good friends.

Around her neck Ruby was wearing the button dangling from a blue ribbon, her Christmas gift from Rita. As pumpkin pie was being served for dessert, she slipped it off the ribbon and held it up for all to see.

"I'm going to pass this around," she told them, "and I want y'all to tell me what you think it is."

As the button went around nobody could make an intelligent guess—except for Bird.

"I seen one of these when I was a young'un," he said. "Seen it with my own eyes."

"Do you know what it is?" Ruby asked.

"Sure. It's a piece of eight!"

That shut everybody up for a second while the guests looked at one another with puzzled eyes. None of them had ever come across a piece of eight. Had the old man really seen one?

"A man gave it to Rita," Ruby told them. "A stranger."

Miss Arbutus caught Ruby's eye. They exchanged a meaningful look as both remembered what Jethro had said in Miss Arbutus's dream—that a stranger would come along and make Ruby's birthday wish come true.

"Could I see it again?" Mr. Crawford asked, and Ruby passed the coin back to him. He held it up to the window light behind him. "What do *you* think it is, Ruby?"

"I'm not sure, but I think Bird is right. It's a piece of eight," Ruby said.

With much ado Bird clambered to his feet and bowed. Then he beamed at the people around the table. Everybody chuckled good-naturedly, and he plopped back into his chair.

"Maybe," Ruby continued, "it's a part of the treasure of Way Down Deep."

Of course laughter followed that remark, as if Ruby were a comedian and this was the funniest punch line in her act. Still they asked to see the coin again. Ruby passed it around for the second time, then a third time, while doing a slow burn at the various negative comments.

Lucy: "Do you think there really *is* a treasure?"

Mr. Crawford: "No, it's just a legend."

Lucy: "Nothing but a fairy tale?"

Mr. Crawford: "Yes. I think every old town has a story like this one."

Robber Bob: "It makes a good bedtime tale for kids."

Miss Duke could stay quiet no longer. "Well, I, for one, believe there *is* a treasure. I felt it in my heart the first time I heard the story."

Everybody stopped talking and turned to her.

"Why would you laugh at a little girl's hopes and dreams?" Miss Duke said. "Because you have no imagination and you have forgotten how to dream yourself."

"I agree!" Peter said.

"And so do I!" Grandma said.

The stream of negativity was stopped in its tracks, and the conversation stalled for a few minutes.

"Does anybody have an idea who this stranger might be?" Miss Duke asked after a while.

All eyes went to Rita, who was sitting beside Miss Arbutus eating her pumpkin pie.

"He was a cowboy," Rita said matter-of-factly.

"A cowboy?" Ruby said. "Why do you say that?"

"He was wearing cowboy boots."

Give her time, Ruby thought, and Rita would remember more details.

Mr. Crawford rolled his eyes as if he were the only person in the room with any sense. But he wouldn't go on about it. Let them have their pipe dreams.

The week after Christmas Ruby and Tripod spent hours scouring the area around The Roost, the neighborhood, then the hills and woods surrounding Way Down, looking for any sign or clue of the treasure.

"Archibald Ward could have hidden his pirate's booty just about anywhere," she said to Peter during morning break on the day they went back to school, "because in the earliest days of Way Down nobody owned the land."

"Wouldn't he have made a marker of some kind?" Peter speculated. "An arrow maybe, or a cross?"

"I haven't seen anything like that," Ruby said.

"What about a map?"

"I don't think so," Ruby said. "Somebody would have found it by this time."

"Yeah, or it could have been destroyed over the years."

"I wish you could help me look," Ruby said.

"Maybe I can help some," Peter said, "but Cedar will have to look after Bird and the kids by himself."

"You should flatter him a bit," Ruby said. "Tell him how grown-up he's acting. Tell him he seems more mature since he quit cussing."

Peter grinned. "Yeah, Cedar likes to feel grown-up."

"It would not be a lie," Ruby said. "He does seem more responsible."

"It's worth a try," Peter said.

And so it was on the following Saturday that Ruby and Peter began an earnest quest for the fabled treasure of Way Down Deep. Their first move was to draw a rough map of the town and surrounding area, and mark it off in sections. They would walk over one section at a time, step by step. They would scrutinize familiar landmarks as they had never done before. After finishing the map, they climbed a hill, sat down, and looked out over the town.

"First, let me tell you what I think about the twinkling man and the man who saved Tripod," Ruby said.

"You think they're one and the same?" Peter said.

"Yes! And if he actually placed Tripod in your yard, that means that he made an appearance twice in the same place."

"You're right," Peter said. "Once to give Rita the coin and once to bring the dog."

"And he had the piece of eight, so he possibly knows where the rest of the treasure is," Ruby said.

"Maybe it's in our yard," Peter said. "Or somewhere close."

"And maybe it's not buried at all!" Ruby added. "Because if there's one coin floating around loose, there may be others."

Thus they began their search at the spot where Rita had seen the cowboy. For the entire morning and half the afternoon they poked and prodded around the yard, underneath the porch and house, and in the bushes. They studied the property from all different angles. Bird, Cedar, the twins, and Rita came out to watch and give advice, and the neighbors came out to learn what was going on. When they found out, they had a good laugh and went back inside.

Of them all, only Bird said anything helpful. "Once upon a time, this house wadn't even standing here."

Peter and Ruby stopped in their tracks to look at him. Of course. That was true of every building in Way Down. Shucks. The treasure could be under the very foundation of any one of them.

Encouraged by Bird's moment of clarity, Cedar said, "We could help, you know. Me and Bird and Skeeter and Jeeter, and Rita, too. We won't make fun of you."

"Thanks, Cedar," Ruby said. "But I think we're through here."

She went to bed that night feeling overwhelmed with the

enormity of this search. She and Peter could spend years poking and prodding and digging and still not find the gold doubloons and pieces of eight. They needed a different strategy. Yes, they would have to use their minds and imaginations instead of wasting their time on footwork.

On Sunday she was not surprised to learn that Peter had come to the same conclusion.

"We gotta concentrate," he said. "Put ourselves in that time and place, and into Archibald's head. Try to think like he thought."

They went back to their hillside spot to get a good view of the town again. But no great flash of enlightenment came that day, nor in the weeks to come. Trying to read the mind of Archibald Ward was harder than poking and prodding around. Even Tripod seemed to grow weary of the weekend searches.

"It just seems so hopeless," Peter said one day. "Such a big area and so many years gone by."

"I now tend to believe it is in the ground after all," Ruby said. "Otherwise, it would have been found by now."

"Yeah, and we could dig up the whole town and still miss that one spot where it's buried," Peter said.

"Let's take a break," Ruby suggested. "Try again in the spring. Maybe in the meantime something will just pop into our heads."

"Or maybe we'll run into the twinkling man again," said Peter. "He got that piece of eight from somewhere. He's our best clue yet."

"Our *only* clue," Ruby said with a sigh.

15

AT FIRST THE MINE CLOSINGS BROUGHT HARDSHIP ONLY TO the miners themselves. Then, as 1955 rolled along, others began to feel the pinch. In late January, due to a shortage in revenue, public services had to be cut back. Way Down's street sweeper, who was Becky's dad, was the first to lose his job. The trash collector, also from Shimpock, was next. More casualties of the crisis were janitors and other maintenance personnel for public places.

In early February the skating rink and bowling alley closed, and The Boxcar Grill cut back to serving only on weekends. The Silver Screen considered closing but instead cut the price of admission. They were barely getting by. Gas went down to seventeen cents a gallon because nobody could pay the national average of twenty-one cents. Mr. Bevins at the barbershop said people's hair had grown so long he didn't recognize a single soul walking down the street. Mrs. Shortt at the hardware store started giving away kerosene heaters because she couldn't sell them, but the people who took them home couldn't afford the fuel to run them. Salesmen stopped lodging at The Roost because they couldn't sell anything in Way Down, and Miss Arbutus started serving a lot of brown beans because she had to cut back on meat and chicken.

Mr. Doctor, however, whose practice had never interfered with his afternoon nap, became disgruntled when he suddenly had more patients backed up than he had chairs in his waiting room.

"All this confounded sickness is the result of money problems," he complained to Cedar, who sometimes came in to help clean up. "Worry and anxiety weaken the body's defenses."

"Like when I had cussitis?" Cedar said. "You told me it was because I had so much hurt eatin' at me inside."

"Something like that," Mr. Doctor said with a smile. He was glad Cedar had understood his meaning even if he didn't remember his exact words.

"Or maybe it's more like when I'm not ready to take a test in Miss Duke's English class, I get a bellyache?"

"Exactly like that," Mr. Doctor said. "The body reacts to stress in many ways. That's why people who live in poverty, along with all their other troubles, have to deal with poor health as well."

Of course the drugstore business was also booming as people poured in with Mr. Doctor's prescriptions, many of which were filled on credit by the kindhearted Morgans.

But the thing that irritated the evangelizing triplets and just about everybody else was that The Beer Barrel was making record profits in this economic slump. In fact, they had more business than they could handle. To see poor men spending precious pennies on strong drink was such an aggravation to some people that they decided to put a stop to it. One Saturday night when the place was packed with drinkers, the Way Down Women's League suddenly stormed into the bar and, with brooms flying, angrily drove all the customers away.

"You got hungry mouths to feed at home!" ninety-year-old Mrs. Rife yelled as she swatted one of the men on the butt with her broom.

"And here you are spending your last dime on the devil's brew!" shouted Mrs. Bevins.

"If you're not ashamed of yourself, you're a clump of dirt!" Mrs. Farmer barked at them.

The men raised their arms across their faces in self-defense, but they did not protest against the women. They moved toward the door as ordered, leaving their beers on the bar. Once outside, a few men lurked in the shadows, hoping to reenter when the women were gone, but much to their dismay the ladies fortified the saloon doors and dared anybody to try to go in.

"We'll be standing here till the sun comes up!" one of the women cried.

"Or till the doors on this sorry establishment are locked and barred!" Mrs. Shortt bellowed.

"Till doomsday, if necessary," Mrs. Morgan added.

Like guilty dogs with their tails tucked between their legs, the men slunk away. A few of them had cars, and others had hitched rides with them. But most had come on foot, and they began the melancholy trek toward home, where they were sure to find their wives on the same warpath as the Way Down Women's League.

"And don't think we're through here!" Mrs. Mullins hollered after them. "You come back, and we come back. You heah me?"

The proprietor of The Beer Barrel quietly locked the doors and cleaned up after his customers, thinking that now he was in the same boat as the rest of the town—busted.

Ruby had always been a big reader, but now she found that she was reading twice as much as usual to keep her mind off sad situations. She soon found she had read all of her own books, and every one on the shelves in the common room. In addition, Miss Duke had been very generous with her books. When there was nothing left at home to read, she decided to go and see if Mrs. Gentry at the public library had something new and interesting.

When Ruby brought her books to the desk to be checked out, she and Mrs. Gentry embraced.

"And how are you and Mr. Gentry getting along out there in your new house?" Ruby asked her.

"It's simply divine, Ruby," she said. "Albeit somewhat isolated."

"Isolated?"

"Yes, I feel so severed from my old friends that I get quite despondent."

"Then you and Mr. Gentry must come for dinner one night."

"That would be exquisite. I'll speak to Mr. Gentry tonight."

"Mrs. Gentry, do you have a book about unemployment?"

Mrs. Gentry's brow wrinkled. "Umemployment? Why would you request such a tome?"

"I want to see if I can find out how people get by without having a job."

"Oh, I see," Mrs. Gentry said. "You are apprehensive for the miners?"

"Yeah, the kids are real sad. I wish I could do something to help. I thought there might be a book."

"Perhaps there is somewhere," Mrs. Gentry said kindly as she stamped the due dates in the two books of fiction Ruby had chosen. "But not in our minuscule collection. Our resources are deficient."

"Yeah, it seems like nobody has enough money these days," Ruby said.

"You're quite right. The mining industry keeps the whole region afloat financially," Mrs. Gentry explained. "And the miners' offspring won't have the opportunity to be anything more than their parents. So you can see the gargantuan value of an education."

"What does that mean?" Ruby asked.

"Well, if these people were educated, or at least trained for other work, they wouldn't have to depend on the capriciousness of the mines."

"Capri . . . what?"

"Fickleness," Mrs. Gentry said. "Mines working one day, closing the next. Opening, closing. They never know when they will have an income."

"And now other businesses are closing," Ruby said.

"Yes, we are all connected that way, as in a web," Mrs. Gentry said. "Economic hardship is like a virus. When it infects one group, all groups in the web are infected."

"At least the library is still open," Ruby said.

Mrs. Gentry gave her a sad smile. "Yes, until the first of May, my dear. That's our date of termination. If things don't turn around, we will be forced to close the library for insufficient funds."

16

O N February 20, in *The Way Down Deep Daily*, The
Roost was the featured business establishment. Morgan's
Drugs, Rife's Five and Dime, and The Boxcar Grill, among
others, had been previous subjects of the Sunday series. This
article was quite lengthy and went into the Ward family history, most of which Ruby knew already from Miss Arbutus.

There were lots of photographs, many showing the building
itself as it evolved over the years. The most recent one was
taken by none other than Slim Morgan, who was given credit
for his work under the picture. There was also a photo of the
sign behind The Roost taken thirty years ago. This sign, however, did not say WAY UP THAT-A-WAY. It said WAY DOWN DEEP.
Under the picture the caption read that for many years—nobody
knew how many—such a sign had stood there. This information
was new to Ruby. In all her stories about the town, Miss Arbutus had not mentioned that the sign used to say something else.

The article went on to report that it had been Miss Arbutus's
grandfather who had expressed the opinion that the sign was

misplaced and inappropriate for that particular spot. So he had changed it to say WAY UP THAT-A-WAY to indicate the path leading to the settlement on the mountain where the Butler clan had lived for a hundred years.

Toward the end of the article there was a photo of Miss Arbutus dressed in her finest ashes-of-roses silk dress. She looked like a rose herself.

Miss Duke read the article to Grandma, who hadn't the patience to struggle through it, and as the other residents gathered round to listen, she suggested they buy several copies of this issue of the paper to keep on display in the common room for traveling guests to see.

The second new thing Ruby learned from the article was that the first building ever built in Way Down was a one-room cabin, constructed by Archibald Ward, the founder of the town, for his wife, on this very spot where The Roost now stood.

At some point between midnight and dawn Ruby woke up with the uneasy feeling that there was something she needed urgently to do. She lay in bed looking at her window, running through a list of possibilities. Had she fed Tripod? Had she watered the houseplants? Had she done her homework? Yes, yes, and yes.

Finally Ruby's mind went back to the newspaper article. Archibald Ward and his family had once lived right here—not in this building, but on this piece of ground. And yes, it was true in those days you didn't own the land until . . . until . . . you built your house on it. Or farmed it. Then it was yours. So if this spot of land belonged to Archibald Ward, he would have buried his treasure here, for why would he have buried it anywhere else?

Ruby knew every square inch of The Roost and the plot of land on which it stood, and there was nothing to indicate that a treasure was buried here. Of course, that didn't mean it wasn't so. Maybe she had missed some important clue. Tomorrow she would start an inch-by-inch search of the grounds.

But she was wide awake now. Why wait until tomorrow? Why not go outside and at least take a look around? She might notice something in the dark that she never noticed in daylight. Yeah, why not? If she ran into anybody, she would tell them that Tripod needed to go.

Without turning on a light she put on her socks and shoes, then found a coat and slipped it over her flannel pajamas. As she lifted Tripod out of his box, he looked at her curiously, as if to say, "What's up? Where we going to?" but he didn't make a sound. She tiptoed down the stairs and into the kitchen. Nobody in sight, not even Miss Arbutus's dream spirit.

She crept out the back door and set Tripod on the porch. Her wagon was stored here along with gardening supplies, a toolbox, and other odds and ends. Tripod went down the steps and started sniffing for critters. Ruby looked around the fenced yard. There was the woodpile that Jethro used to climb, but nothing else of interest was to be seen here.

How much of this land had Archibald Ward claimed for himself? The same plot that now belonged to Miss Arbutus?

Probably. Her land extended as far as the WAY UP THAT-A-WAY sign. Ruby went out the gate and walked to the sign. Why had it once read WAY DOWN DEEP? This was an odd place for a sign with the town's name on it—behind a building. Why had it been here? Might the words have had a double meaning? Could it have meant that the treasure was buried way down deep right where the sign stood? On the flat grassy spot where they had buried Jethro? Surely not. That was way too easy. *Somebody* would have figured it out over the years, wouldn't they?

And if that was the case, the grave diggers would have found the treasure. Unless . . . unless they didn't dig far enough. Jethro's grave was kind of shallow, just deep enough for the broom-straw basket to be well covered.

What if Archibald made the sign and placed it on that spot in order to say to his descendants, "The treasure is here—way down deep," but nobody paid attention? All her life she had heard it: *The treasure is buried way down deep somewhere here in Way Down Deep.*

Suddenly a rush of exhilaration raced up her spine, into her brain, and made her scalp prickle. Yes! The treasure was in the ground underneath Jethro! She had never been more certain of anything.

Inside her pocket was a pair of gloves. She slipped them on before she hurried to the back porch again and grabbed a shovel.

What about the ground? It was still winter. Would it be frozen? She walked to the grave and jabbed the shovel into the

114

dirt. Good! The earth here was loose, perhaps from the grave. She began to dig. Then she became aware that Tripod had started to dig right beside her. Having only three paws to work with didn't seem to be a problem.

"Thanks, my friend," she said to him in the dark.

Dirt flew everywhere, into Ruby's hair, down the collar and up the sleeves of her coat, into her eyes and mouth and ears. Tripod was covered and his paws were caked.

"Just a little more," she whispered again and again in the black night. "Just a little deeper."

After a while, she threw the coat aside and continued working in her pajamas. Then she ran into the broom-straw basket. She had to admit that she couldn't possibly lift it out by herself. It had taken four boys to lower it into the hole. She would stop for a rest and think. She and Tripod sat together on the ground breathing heavily.

"We have to finish before daylight, Tripod," Ruby said. "People will look at me funny. Not Miss Arbutus, or Miss Duke or Grandma, but others. They'll think I've gone crazy with grief or something, trying to dig up poor Jethro. Or they'll make fun of me. Even some kids will."

She went back to the hole, and Tripod followed. She gave the basket a test tug, and to her surprise, it was easily dislodged from the dirt. In fact, it seemed to be empty. She lifted the lid, but it was too dark to see inside the basket. Cautiously she leaned forward and stretched forth one hand to feel inside. She remembered Cedar falling into the basket on top of Jethro. He had been so disturbed, he had cussed. With that memory she drew her hand back. Could she do this? She had to. She plunged her hand into the basket, and with much relief discovered that it really was empty. But where was Jethro?

She pulled the basket out of the hole and threw it aside. Then she took up her shovel, jumped into the hole, and began to dig again. This ground was harder but not frozen.

Tripod stood above her now, watching curiously. He was trying to figure out how to get down there and help, but it was a steep jump for a small dog.

"You keep watch for me," Ruby said to him. "Tell me if you see anybody."

Tripod agreed. She continued digging. At the very moment when she was so exhausted that she didn't think she could lift her shovel again, she felt something beneath her feet. Something hard and flat. It had four corners. It was rectangular. And it was wedged tightly into the earth. She would have to dig away all the packed dirt from around it. She concentrated on one side at a time until all the dirt was removed and there was a space between the chest and the earth on all sides. Then she struggled with the lid and, in the dark, couldn't figure out how it was fastened.

Ruby sat back on her heels. Her arms and shoulders were aching. When she stood up, her legs wobbled. With the last of her strength she pulled herself out of the hole.

"Tripod," she whispered, "I can't get the chest open to see what's inside, and it's too heavy for me to lift out of the hole. We'll have to get somebody to help us, but I'm too tired to think who'd be strong enough. Let's just lie down right here for a minute and rest."

Ruby wrapped herself in the coat and lay down on the cold brown grass. Her eyes closed. Tripod lay down beside her and closed his eyes, too.

"Just for a minute," she said to Tripod. "One little minute."

Ruby came awake with Tripod licking her face. Her eyes flew open. The chest was sitting on the grass beside her with a cloud of blue mist hanging over it. Tripod was whining, and his tail was wagging like crazy.

"Do you think Baldy was here, Tripod?" she cried excitedly. "Did he lift the chest out of the hole for us?"

She didn't know who was more excited, she or Tripod. She pulled herself up to her knees in front of the chest. In the blue glow she could now see that the lid was secured with two rawhide cords, each one twined around a hook. She raked the dirt away from the cords, worked them loose from the hooks, and tugged at the top. After a few hard jerks it came open. Tripod jumped up and placed his front paws on the rim of the box, balanced on his one good hind leg, and peered curiously inside.

Yes, Ruby thought, it was just as she had dreamed it would be. She ran her fingers through the coins. A chest full of them. She had found the treasure of Way Down Deep!

17

IT WAS MY BIRTHDAY WISH," SHE WHISPERED. "NOW I CAN MAKE the wishes of others come true as well."

Daylight began to tiptoe over an eastern mountaintop as she and Tripod sat there staring at the money.

"Tripod," she said, "listen to me carefully."

Tripod dropped to the ground, tilted his head to one side, and waited for Ruby to speak.

"You have a very important role to play, Tripod. You are the guardian of the treasure of Way Down Deep, and you must protect it with your life until I get back. Okay?"

Tripod walked all the way around the chest, settled down in front of it, and looked at Ruby with inquisitive eyes.

"Oh, you want to know where I'm going?" Ruby said. "I'm going to fetch Miss Arbutus. But I'll be right back."

Tripod glanced around, then tilted his head again and looked at Ruby.

"No, Tripod," she said, "I'm not really worried about anybody stealing the money while I'm gone. Way Down people don't steal. But this . . . this is so . . . so valuable. I wouldn't want to put temptation in front of anybody."

Tripod agreed wholeheartedly. He placed his head on his front paws, happy for the rest.

"Good boy," Ruby said. "I knew I could count on you."

She closed the lid of the chest, then went inside and knocked on Miss Arbutus's door. No answer. Miss Arbutus had taught her never to enter somebody else's bedroom until she heard "Come in." She knocked again. No answer. But this was way too important to stand on protocol. She opened the door and barged in. A very thin thread of light was slipping around the edges of the window curtains, and she could see Miss Arbutus sleeping soundly in her bed. She walked over and shook her shoulder. At first Miss Arbutus did not move at all. Ruby shook harder and spoke.

"Miss Arbutus, please. I'm sorry to disturb you, but please, Miss Arbutus . . . ?"

Miss Arbutus opened her eyes and looked at Ruby, but she didn't seem really to see her. "What? What is it?"

"Please wake up. It's important."

Miss Arbutus sat up, seeming very groggy and out of it. "I was in Spain," she said. "I was at a bullfight, and I felt such pity for that bull. I told the people to leave the poor animal alone. I was crying and pleading with them when I felt you tugging on my shoulder."

"Oh, no!" Ruby groaned. "I'm so sorry for the bull. I really am. Maybe you could have saved him."

"I don't think so, dear," Miss Arbutus said as she wiped away a tear. "The people were laughing at me. I told them it was very wrong to treat animals like that, but . . . but . . . what is it, Ruby? What's the matter?"

"It's the treasure, Miss Arbutus. I have found the treasure of Way Down Deep."

"No, my sweet girl, you were dreaming, too," Miss Arbutus said to her.

"This is *not* a dream," Ruby said, and there was such sincerity in her voice that Miss Arbutus was inclined to believe her.

"Show me, then," Miss Arbutus said, then rose from her bed, dressed in her robe and slippers, and followed Ruby outside.

Tripod was lying right where she had left him, in front of the chest. He stood up and wagged his tail when he saw them approach. Ruby lifted the chest lid for Miss Arbutus to see inside. At that moment the sun sent a splash of brand-new light directly onto the coins. Miss Arbutus gasped and sank to her knees.

"Heavens," she whispered. "Sun, moon, and stars!" She was not as well versed in expletives as some other people Ruby knew.

Ruby started jabbering so fast even she wasn't sure what she was saying.

"And Jethro wasn't there?" Miss Arbutus interrupted when she got to that part.

"No, he was gone."

Miss Arbutus looked at the empty basket, which Ruby had tossed aside. "What in the name of heaven?"

Ruby went on with the story of her night's adventure.

"How do you think the chest got out of the hole?" Miss Arbutus interrupted her again.

"I don't know, but I think maybe . . . I don't know," Ruby said. "I'll have to think about that."

When she was finished, Miss Arbutus remained kneeling on the ground in her robe, stunned and amazed, staring at the treasure.

Ruby ran to the porch for her Radio Flyer and pulled it up beside the chest.

"Let's load it into the wagon," she said to Miss Arbutus.

"Why? Where are you taking it?"

"To Mayor Chambers! And you gotta go with me. We're giving it to the people of Way Down. Don't you see, Miss Arbutus? This was meant to be. The treasure has come at a time when the town needs it the most."

Miss Arbutus felt such a great swelling of pride in her heart at that moment that she couldn't even speak. She simply nodded and rose to her feet. Ruby closed the chest again, and together they struggled to move it, but between the two of them they could lift it only an inch off the ground.

"Ruby," Miss Arbutus said. "I think this is what we should do. We will fetch Mr. Crawford, and ask him to help us load the chest onto the wagon. Then you should take the treasure to the mayor by yourself."

"By myself? Why?"

"You found it all by yourself, and you should present it to

the town by yourself. This is your moment, not mine, not anybody else's."

"Peter should go with me," Ruby said. "He tried so hard. And Tripod helped me dig."

"Of course. They should both go with you. I'll call Peter for you. Perhaps Tripod should ride on top of the chest."

They smiled at each other in the sparkling light of morning.

"I'll also wake Mr. Crawford," Miss Arbutus said. "You get dressed."

Ruby looked down at herself. She was caked with dirt from head to toe, but she wouldn't take time for a bath. She would just change into her dungarees.

"I'll be right back," she said, and hurried to her room.

When she returned, Miss Arbutus was standing with Mr. Crawford on the back porch.

"I left a message with Robber Bob to send Peter over," Miss Arbutus said. "But I didn't say why."

Mr. Crawford was also in his robe and house slippers, seeming irritated and half asleep.

"What's going on?" he grumbled.

"Let's show him," Miss Arbutus said to Ruby.

"Yeah, let's do!" Ruby said with a grin. "Let's show him!"

She was thinking of how he had been so flippant about the treasure at the Christmas dinner. She and Miss Arbutus walked quickly to the chest, while Mr. Crawford trailed behind.

"What is it?" he said as he looked at the hole in the ground, then at the chest.

"Behold the treasure of Way Down Deep," Miss Arbutus said to him. "Our own Ruby and Tripod found it."

"Oh, sure," Mr. Crawford said with a yawn. "No, really, what's this all about?"

Ruby and Miss Arbutus, both with hands on hips, just stood there staring at him, and the realization dawned on him that neither the woman nor the girl was cracking a smile, as one might do if one were trying to pull your leg.

"We need you to help us lift the chest onto Ruby's wagon," Miss Arbutus said. "Please?"

Mr. Crawford looked from one of them to the other. What *was* going on here?

"Do you mind?" Miss Arbutus asked politely.

"M-may I look inside the box?" Mr. Crawford asked, stammering a little.

"One tiny peek," Ruby said. "And you can't tell anybody."

Ruby raised the lid of the chest. Mr. Crawford leaned forward and gazed at the contents, then let out several strange guttural sounds, but nothing that would pass for human speech.

Ruby dissolved into a giggling fit.

"Now will you help us?" Miss Arbutus said, closing the chest again.

He stared at the closed chest as if he were in a state of shock.

"Uh . . . is he okay?" Ruby asked.

"He'll come round in a minute," was Miss Arbutus's reply.

Mr. Crawford found his voice at last. "I don't think . . . I don't think . . . we can lift it. We need more help."

As if on cue, the milk truck could be heard lumbering to a stop at the curb. The four of them walked around the side of the building just as Mr. Stacey, the milkman, dressed in his spotless dairyman's whites, stepped out of the truck and onto the sidewalk, carrying Miss Arbutus's order.

"I'm late! I'm late!" he cried, which reminded Ruby of the big white rabbit in *Alice in Wonderland*.

"No," Miss Arbutus replied. "You're right on time as always."

18

As the two men, Miss Arbutus, Ruby, and Tripod were going back around the corner of the building, Bird, who had slipped away from his family, appeared on the sidewalk. There was something in the hushed conversation of this group that tweaked his curiosity, so he followed them and became a witness to the heaving of the chest onto the wagon. He overheard the words "gold doubloons" and "pieces of eight."

A moment later Lucy, Grandma, and Miss Duke stepped out onto the porch. Jude, the new typesetter, who also delivered the paper on Ward Street while on his way home from work each morning, was tending to that chore when he saw the three ladies walking around the building. Being curious, he also followed. He overheard the word "treasure."

"What's going on?" Jude said to the ladies. "What has happened?"

"We think Ruby has found the treasure," Miss Duke said.

"No foolin'?" Jude said excitedly. "Do you think we can see it?"

But nobody could see it now. Ruby was taking it to the mayor. She and Miss Arbutus tied the rawhide cords securely. Then Ruby began pulling the Radio Flyer loaded with the chest across the grass toward the sidewalk. She discovered that the wagon was difficult to manuever with so much weight on it. Still in a state of bewilderment, Mr. Crawford tried to help her. His hair was disheveled and his robe had come undone, so he repeatedly tramped on it with wet slippers. Mr. Stacey was also trying to help, and in the process his white outfit was no longer white. Even after she had reached the pavement, Ruby found that the wagon was too unwieldy to manipulate.

Then it seemed like a silent signal went out into the community, because more and more people started arriving at The Roost.

"Ruby did what?"

"Where at?"

"In the ground?"

"You gotta' be foolin'."

As more folks gathered, Miss Arbutus quietly slipped away and went back to her room to dress for the day, but Miss Duke, Grandma, and Lucy stayed to watch the show. Some people were falling all over themselves to help Ruby guide the wagon, and she kept saying no. She and Peter were going to do this. At that moment she saw him pushing his way through the crowd.

"There you are," she called to him. "Come help me."

"Sure! Let's move it over to the street," Peter said breathlessly. "I know it's the treasure, right?"

Ruby grinned and nodded as they guided the wagon onto the street. Yes, it rolled easier there.

Mr. Crawford went inside to get dressed and Mr. Stacey reluctantly went back to his milk truck to finish his deliveries, only to realize there were so many people in the street he couldn't drive away. So, for the first time in his life, he abandoned his duties and happily joined this adventure to wherever it might lead him.

Sheriff Reynolds arrived on the scene. "What's going on here?"

By this time most of the town was in the street, on the sidewalk, or on the lawn and porch of The Roost watching the goings-on.

"We will need a police escort, sir," Ruby said to Sheriff Reynolds. "Our cargo is quite valuable."

The sheriff, who had a lot of heart but few smarts, actually turned to the people in the street and gave them an exaggerated wink. Then he turned back to her.

"An escort, huh? Whatever you say, Miss Ruby. I'm here to serve."

Ruby picked Tripod up and set him on top of the chest. Tripod looked around at the people, then lay down and rested his head on his paws. He was pretty well tuckered out.

Judge Elbert Deel, having arrived the night before, stepped onto the front porch of The Roost and saw the crowd gathered round Ruby. He was immediately reminded of the morning she had first appeared in Way Down Deep.

"What's happening?" the judge asked Lantha, the teenage daughter of the Bevinses, who ran the barbershop.

"Ruby found the treasure!" Lantha said.

"What treasure?" Judge Deel said.

"The treasure of Way Down Deep, sir," Lantha gushed. "Can you believe it?"

Well, of course she did, Judge Deel was thinking. If there was a treasure to be found, who else but Ruby would find it?

The sheriff led the way, followed by Ruby and Peter with the wagon and chest, and Tripod on top sound asleep. The crowd managed to control itself and stay at a respectful distance.

Jude had pulled out a pad of paper and tried to write the story, but he soon discovered he did not have the ability. It wasn't as easy as one might think. So he had run to the office of the editor of *The Way Down Deep Daily*, who should have been the first person in Ruby's entourage but was instead sleeping on the couch in his office.

"If you wanna get the scoop of the century," Jude had yelled in order to wake him up, "it's happening on Ward Street!"

So now the editor was in the crowd following Ruby. He threw out questions as they went along and jotted down the answers as best he could while walking. The longer this went on, the more confused the sheriff became. At first he had considered this whole thing some kind of a prank, but here was the editor of the paper, and Mr. Dales, who was the bank president, preachers and schoolteachers, and nearly everybody else in Way Down following this girl with her wagon down the street. About the time the crowd reached the courthouse, where the mayor's office was, it appeared that all the schoolchildren were arriving, too. Maybe he should take this a bit more seriously?

"Clear the way," he began to say in a deep, authoritative voice as he pushed imaginary obstacles out of the path. "Clear the way for . . . for . . . Yes, clear the way."

Mayor Chambers, having been alerted to the crowd coming his way, met them outside on the sidewalk.

"I heard . . . but I . . ." he said to Ruby when she pulled the wagon up in front of him. "I don't know what to say."

He really didn't know what to say, because he certainly couldn't believe what he had heard. Yet here were all these people . . .

Ruby set Tripod on the pavement. Then with Peter's help she opened the chest and showed the treasure to the mayor. There were gasps and expressions of surprise and small screams of delight as the people jostled one another and went into all manner of contortions in order to gaze upon the long-dreamed-of treasure.

The mayor was struck dumb, and Sheriff Reynolds collapsed to the curb. Then the mayor landed right beside him. Flashbulbs were popping all over the place as Slim Morgan also saw the scoop of a lifetime. He took pictures of Ruby, Tripod, and Peter with the chest, the sheriff and the mayor on the curb, and the people with their mouths open and their eyes shining.

"Mr. Mayor," Ruby said, and the crowd fell silent and listened. As she pushed the red curls away from her face, a big clump of dirt fell out of her hair onto the pavement. Ruby and everybody else stared at the clod on the sidewalk for a moment before Ruby shrugged and went on. "Mr. Mayor, I hereby present this treasure to the people of Way Down Deep."

19

RUBY WAS IMMEDIATELY HOISTED INTO THE AIR AMID CHEERS and tears and singing in the streets. She found herself suspended above the crowd as it followed Peter and the sheriff pulling the wagon and chest with Tripod now sitting up grinning at the delighted humans. He would have taken a bow had he known how. The ensuing traffic jam involved almost a dozen vehicles as the people swarmed down Busy Street. At the doorway of the bank Ruby was set onto her feet again. That establishment had not yet opened for business, but Mr. Dales invited Ruby, Peter, and Tripod in, along with the sheriff, Mr. Chambers, and several members of the city council. There he made a big production of locking the chest inside a vault.

"When can the people have their money?" Ruby asked.

"As soon as possible, Ruby," Mr. Chambers said. "Mr. Dales will safeguard it here in the vault until it can be converted to U.S. dollars and spent according to the town's good judgment."

"Perhaps our initial move should be to call in a coin expert," the banker said. "I have heard of one in Washington, D.C. We could have him come over here and evaluate the coins and give us a rough idea of how much money we are dealing with."

"That's a good plan," Ruby said. "Then what?"

"That's up to you and the mayor," Mr. Dales said.

Ruby turned to the mayor.

"I move," the mayor said, "that, as soon as we have an estimate, we call a town meeting and hear suggestions from the people."

"Agreed," chorused the bank president and the city council members.

The group stepped outside and announced these decisions to the folks in the street.

The crowd clapped and cheered.

"Then can we have a celebration?" Ruby asked.

"Yeah!" Peter said excitedly. "A big old party for the whole town?"

Everybody laughed long and loud. Of course they would have laughed at almost anything. They were as giddy as giggling babies.

"Yes!" the mayor agreed. "We will have a bash the likes of which Way Down has never seen before."

That's when the cheers went up so loudly they echoed against the mountains and resounded throughout the valley.

"But now I'm sorry to say," the mayor finished up, "that for the time being, we must all go to work. It is, after all, a Monday morning. To make your day go quickly, you can hold it in your minds and hearts that you have been a witness to an important historic event this morning. May God bless you all."

The people hugged one another and laughed some more, and shed a few tears of joy. Yes, it was a moment never to be forgotten. It was another hour before Ruby reached home again, as she was stopped a dozen or more times to be questioned, congratulated, patted on the back, or hugged. Tripod rode sleeping in the wagon, and Peter walked beside them, along with others who were going their way.

"I guess we'd better go to school, then, huh?" Peter said without enthusiasm as they reached The Roost. The school bell had rung long ago.

"I'm going to ask Miss Arbutus if I can stay home," Ruby said with a yawn. "I don't think I can hold my eyes open any longer."

With more hullabaloo from The Roost residents, it was another half hour before Ruby was able to ask Miss Arbutus if she could skip school and rest. She said okay, as Ruby had known she would, and Grandma and Lucy agreed to look after Tripod while she slept. She took a long bath, then dressed in clean pajamas and went back to bed to sleep most of the day away. Her dreams were filled with visions of pirates and one swashbuckling hero with the unromantic name of Baldy.

Mr. and Mrs. Gentry arrived for supper that evening as previously arranged by Miss Arbutus. Everybody bustled into the dining room, chattering with excitement.

"What are we eating tonight?" Rita asked.

"Fried chicken," Miss Arbutus said happily, and kissed the little girl on the head. Even she seemed more animated and joyful on this day.

"Just like old times," Mr. Gentry said as he looked at the spread on the table.

"Please, Ruby," Mrs. Gentry said as the food was being passed around, "convey the minutiae."

"Do what?" Ruby said.

"She means spill the details," Mr. Gentry explained.

So Ruby told the story once again and was surprised that she was not interrupted even once.

"Who would believe it?" Lucy said. "All those decades, even centuries, and the treasure was right there under a sign that told everybody it was there!"

"They were not tuned in," Grandma said. "But our smart girl, Ruby, figured it out even after the sign was changed. She's just like her mother, you know, like my Jolene." Grandma's voice broke and she wiped impatiently at her eyes.

"Do you think Mama would have found the treasure?" Ruby asked wistfully. "I mean, if she were here and still alive?"

"Definitely," Grandma said. "She was curious about everything, and as smart as they come, that one. You do her proud."

Mr. Crawford spoke up. "Ruby, I want to apologize to you for being such a wet blanket at the Christmas dinner. I'll have to say you proved me wrong, and I'm glad you did, for I have learned never again to make fun of someone else's dreams."

"Oh, that's okay, Mr. Crawford," Ruby said, not being one

to hold a grudge. "It was my birthday wish. When I started to blow out my candles, it just popped into my head that I would like to find the treasure. So that's what I wished for."

"You must write this up and send it to your editor to add to the book," Miss Duke said to Mr. Crawford.

"You are quite right, my dear," he said. "After all, it's the most important event that has happened in Way Down since the founding of the town."

20

THE VERY NEXT DAY THE MAYOR CALLED MISS ARBUTUS AND asked her and Ruby to meet him at the bank. The coin expert had arrived. Miss Arbutus took Ruby from school and they walked to the bank, where a stern-faced man dressed in a fancy suit was waiting in the lobby, impatiently tapping his foot. Ruby, on hearing the man's name, thought it was so strange and complicated that she dubbed him Mr. Expert on the spot. Mr. Chambers, being quite nervous in the presence of a Washington, D.C., big shot, actually forgot to introduce Ruby and Miss Arbutus by name.

"We're sorry to keep you waiting," Miss Arbutus apologized to Mr. Expert. "Ruby was in the midst of a history test and could not get away until now."

Mr. Expert said nothing, just rolled his eyes toward Mr. Dales, who stood by ready to show the coins. Mr. Dales quickly ushered the mayor, Mr. Expert, Miss Arbutus, and Ruby toward the vault in an atmosphere of tension.

As Mr. Dales struggled with the combination lock, Mr. Expert reminded him, "I do have a train to catch at three p.m."

"Oh, you have plenty of time," Ruby chimed in pleasantly with a big smile. "Besides, the engineer will wait for you if you call ahead and tell him you'll be late."

Mr. Expert rolled his eyes again. Ruby shrugged. Mr. Dales rotated the wheel on the vault and swung the door open. Once inside the vault, Mr. Dales fumbled hopelessly with the cords and hooks on the chest until Ruby came to his aid. Then she flung the lid open, and there were the coins glittering under the electric lights like thousands of twinkling stars.

"Well now," Mr. Expert said as he knelt to examine the booty.

For a moment there was silence as they waited to hear what Mr. Expert had to say. Of the four of them only Ruby was completely relaxed. She knew what the findings would be.

Mr. Expert held what appeared to be a jeweler's eyeglass to one of his eyes and picked up coins one by one for examination.

"Well now!" he said again, more forcefully this time. "What have we here?"

Ruby smiled at Mayor Chambers.

"OH . . . MY . . . GOODNESS!" Mr. Expert suddenly declared in a very loud voice, emphasizing each word. "I have never . . . I have never . . . Oh, for heaven's sake, look at THAT! Oh my goodness!"

After several of these exclamations, he disregarded his expensive suit, fell down on his bottom in front of the chest, and began to dig through the coins as Tripod would dig for a bone.

"I can't believe it! I can't believe it! I am amazed. What . . . ? Where? Upon my word!"

Now the mayor, Mr. Dales, and Miss Arbutus were smiling along with Ruby.

"Unbelievable!" was Mr. Expert's final word as he dropped all the coins back into place and simply sat there staring at them for the longest time.

"So how much?" Ruby blurted out. "A couple thousand dollars maybe?"

Mr. Expert jerked his head around to face her. "You are the child who found it, right? You are Ruby?"

Ruby bobbed her head up and down as she grinned at him. "Yes, sir!"

For the first time he smiled. "Well, Ruby, what you have here are *some* pieces of eight, but mostly gold doubloons—very, very old ones dating from the mid–sixteen hundreds through the early seventeen hundreds. Each one has a different value according to its date and condition, but I can promise you that altogether they are worth much more than a couple thousand dollars."

"How much, then?" Ruby persisted.

Mr. Expert stood up and smoothed down his clothing before answering. "I can't give you an exact figure, but I'm confident their worth will go into the millions."

Mr. Chambers gasped and slumped against the wall. His face had gone red.

"Are you all right?" Ruby asked him, and touched his arm.

"You do look flushed, sir," Miss Arbutus said.

Then she and Mr. Dales helped the mayor outside of the vault and to the reception area, where they eased him onto the genuine leatherette sofa.

Mr. Expert took a last wistful look at the coins and followed.

"I'm all right," the mayor said as Shelby Chambers, his daughter-in-law and one of the bank tellers, brought him a glass of water. "I'm just so overwhelmed with joy for my people."

"And well you should be," Mr. Expert said as he sat down on the couch beside Mr. Chambers. Ruby and Miss Arbutus sat in the matching leatherette chairs.

"Lock the vault, please, Shelby," Mr. Dales instructed his teller, then sat in another chair.

Shelby locked the vault, then disappeared into a back room. Ruby hoped she was going for cookies, since she knew it was the custom of the bank to serve them for special guests.

Mr. Expert thoughtfully studied each of their faces before saying, "My immediate concern is that someone will try to cheat you. I'm sure you're aware there are unscrupulous people out there. So you must protect yourselves. First thing to do is hire a good lawyer. And second, let me contact the persons at this address." He plucked a bundle of business cards from the inside pocket of his suit jacket, flipped through them, and handed one to Mr. Dales. "It's a trustworthy exchange in New York City with an excellent reputation. They will not take advantage of you."

Shelby appeared with coffee and cookies. She served Miss Arbutus first, then Mr. Expert. Ruby noticed that he took three cookies. Ruby took only one.

"I'm sorry I'm not current on these matters," Mr. Dales said, "but what will these people do for us?"

"Everything," Mr. Expert said. "I will inform them of the find, and they will do the rest. I'm sure they will come here to evaluate the coins, so you won't have to transport them. And I have no doubt they will be as astonished as I am. Please have your lawyer present when they arrive."

"Then what?" the mayor asked. "Our people need money."

"And they shall have it," Mr. Expert said. "A lot of it. The representatives of this exchange will answer all of your questions and take care of your needs."

"Very good, sir," the mayor said to Mr. Expert. "I don't want to be the cause of your missing the train. Please send me a bill for your services."

"I'm too keyed up now to travel," Mr. Expert said. "In my wildest fantasies I did not expect . . ." He glanced toward the vault and his eyes glazed over. His last cookie remained half eaten in his hand. Then he pulled himself together and smiled at Ruby again. "You see, child, this is a dream come true for a man in my line of work. I am very interested in this story about the treasure, and so enchanted by your town that I don't want to leave. I would also like to view those exquisite coins once more before they are sold off. I thought perhaps that one of you might recommend a place for a weary man to sleep tonight?"

"Indeed I can," the mayor said enthusiastically, and turned to

Miss Arbutus. "This lady is Miss Arbutus Ward, a direct descendant of Archibald Ward, the founder of Way Down Deep, who, according to legend, was the one who buried the treasure. Miss Arbutus is not only Ruby's guardian but also the proprietor of a lovely little boardinghouse called The Roost."

Mr. Expert nodded approvingly at Miss Arbutus. "How quaint," he said. "And do you serve dinner, my lady?"

"Yes, sir. I serve breakfast and supper, as we call it, every day," Miss Arbutus said in her soft Southern voice. "I have a clean room available, and you are welcome to stay."

"Sounds perfect. I am tired and hungry."

"Then don't spoil your appetite with cookies," Ruby scolded. She felt herself blushing a little when the three men chuckled.

"Well, that's what Miss Arbutus always tells me," she said.

"Very good advice," Mr. Expert said, but still he finished off the third cookie.

And that's how the coin man came to be a regular visitor in Way Down. Perhaps Miss Arbutus learned his real name, but to her and Ruby and most everybody else in town he remained Mr. Expert for the rest of his life. During his future visits to The Roost, he lost all of his crabbiness as well as his habit of wearing fancy clothes, and many years later he became an honorary citizen of Way Down Deep.

But that's getting ahead of the story.

Back to that afternoon when Mr. Expert first arrived. The word went out immediately that the treasure was worth millions. The people were so excited they began to dance in the streets, and church bells rang until all hours of the night.

A few days later a team from New York arrived to assess the coins. They agreed wholeheartedly with Mr. Expert. There was a fortune here. With the town's brand-new lawyer from Charleston supervising, the team set about the tedious process of evaluating and cataloging the coins one by one.

21

EVERYBODY AND HIS KIN TURNED OUT FOR THE FIRST MEET-
ing. It was held in the courtroom because it had more
seats than any other place in town. As the citizens entered and
milled about, there was an air of hushed excitement. Ruby sat
in the front row with Miss Arbutus and Grandma. Other children were there as well, sitting with their families. The mayor
called the meeting to order and announced its purpose, as if
the people didn't know already.

"We will open the floor now for suggestions, discussion, and
debate."

Nearly every person in the room stood up and spoke simul-
taneously. Then they all laughed and sat down.

"I think it will be more practical," the mayor said, "if we go
one at a time. We'll pretend we're back in school and raise our
hands for recognition."

Many hands waved, and the mayor called on one person at
a time.

The first suggestion was to place all the money into the

town's general fund and use it as needed. Of course they could first take care of projects that had been waiting in the wings for years, such as repairing the bridge over Deep Creek, renovating the train station and the bus station, and widening Busy Street.

"Those things will eventually get done anyway!" somebody yelled, and knocked that idea down. "We want to do something special with this money."

"Right!"

"Yeah, something exciting!"

"I think we should divide the money equally among the churches of the community," the Presbyterian minister's wife suggested, "so that it will do God's work."

"And who will decide what *is* God's work?"

Nobody answered that question or commented further on the subject, but there was the general feeling that giving the money to God was not a popular idea.

"I suggest we give equal amounts to each citizen of the town," another person said.

There were nods of approval. Best suggestion yet.

"But what is the definition of town?" somebody said.

"Right. Our city limits do not incorporate a lot of people."

"It's true. Much of our community is spread out into the surrounding hollers."

"Should we include Shimpock in the windfall?" somebody asked. "Many of them work in Way Down."

"I think we should. They have been good citizens."

"But they live outside the city limits."

"Then are we establishing a rule that you *have* to live inside the city limits?"

"I'm just making a statement. They don't live inside the city limits."

"Maybe we should include anybody with a Way Down Deep address?"

"That's a good idea."

"But that includes most of the county," Mrs. Farmer said, and she should know. She delivered the mail.

"The mining communities don't have a Way Down address, but I think we should include them anyway. They are having such a hard time right now."

"If we help everybody who needs help, the money will be spread so thin it won't do anybody much good."

"Fair point."

"Besides, the mining communities are too far out. They are not a part of Archibald Ward's town."

"But the mining business has supported this town!" someone yelled.

It was the first indication that people were getting testy.

"Let's stay calm," the mayor said in a soothing voice. "We can do this without raising our voices."

Ruby's heart was beginning to sink. What was happening here? No money for Shimpock? No money for the miners?

"Okay," a calm and reasonable voice spoke up. "We have to draw a line somewhere."

"Yes, I think the money should go only to people who live inside the city limits."

All persons who lived inside the city limits agreed.

"And what about the new houses on Highway 99?" said another. "Those people *used* to live in Way Down, and some of them have businesses here still. What about them?"

"They don't live inside the city limits! We have to draw the line!"

"But the bank president and mayor have built houses out there," someone said. "And they lived in Way Down for years, and still support our community efforts. How can we leave them out?"

"They don't live in Way Down!"

"Let me tell you something!" Mr. Dales said. His patience was wearing thin. "The Reeders live in my house on Ward Street rent-free. So you are saying they can collect the money because they live in town, but I can't?"

It was a good question. Nobody had a good answer.

"If that's the case, then I would just have to put them out on the street and move my own family back into my house!" Mr. Dales said angrily. And he sat down.

This was not going well.

"Yeah, maybe we should include the mayor and the bank president," someone said. Others agreed.

"Are we including the mayor and the bank president just because of who they are?" Mr. Gentry said angrily. "What about other people living out there on Highway 99 who used to live in town, like me and my wife? We lived at The Roost for years and both of us worked in town. We still work here."

"I think we need to adjourn for now and call another meeting for the same time and place tomorrow night," the mayor said.

"Adjourn? We're just getting started!"

"That's what I'm afraid of," the mayor said. "We should go home and cool off. And let's give this thing some serious thought before tomorrow night."

So the Way Down folks went their separate ways, mumbling and grumbling in the night.

The next evening people strolled into the second meeting in a friendly and relaxed manner. They greeted each other with smiles, handshakes, and a few hugs. This time the children all sat together on benches that lined the back wall of the courtroom so that they could make a quick exit if they wanted to. The mayor called the meeting to order.

"I have another suggestion," Mr. Bevins opened. "Why not give a certain amount of money to each business in town so they can expand and hire folks who are out of work?"

"Yeah," someone agreed. "It's called stimulating the economy."

"Good idea," several people said. Of course those several people had businesses in town.

"What qualifies as a business?" someone asked.

"You know what a business is," Mrs. Shortt said. "It's a trade. A place that has goods or services to sell."

"Okay, we know the grocery store is a business. Also the

dime store, the bank, the drugstore, the newspaper, the boarding-house, and so on, all are obviously businesses. What about shoe shining? Is that a business?"

"Is babysitting a business?"

"I sell Avon. Is that a business?"

"Is peddling my garden vegetables a business?"

The consensus was that none of those activities were actually businesses.

"Why not? Who is to decide what is and is not a business?"

"I own a sawmill in Farmer's Ridge," Mr. Farmer said, "at my family's old home place. That's a business. So what about people living in town who have businesses outside of town? Do we get a share for that business?"

"No, the business should be inside the city limits."

"There you go with the city limits thing again."

"Yeah, seems like some people have a fixation on city limits."

"Well, it *is* Archibald Ward's money, and this is his town, you know?"

"I thought it was *our* money!"

"All right, all right," the mayor said. "Don't start again."

"What about the Mullins family?" somebody else piped up. "They own two businesses. Do they get two shares?"

Nobody could answer that one.

"The bank is definitely a business, but why should they get a share when they already have so much money?"

Mr. Dales the banker answered that one. "Simple. I could use it to make low-interest business loans. You know, to help them expand."

"You're going to loan us our own money and charge interest?"

Everybody laughed long and loud, but it was not a pleasant laugh. It was an ugly laugh.

Mr. Dales stormed out of the room.

After another fifteen minutes of that sort of exchange, the mayor adjourned the meeting again. "I'll let you know," he said, "when we'll come together again."

"I heard all that wealth has turned people against one another," Johnny Ray Springstep said to Ruby at school. "That's what happens when money comes into the picture."

"Not really," Ruby said. "We're just having a hard time deciding how to spend it. We'll find the right answer."

"Maybe you should have kept it," Johnny Ray said.

She watched Johnny Ray walk back to his desk. She knew he did not mean to be nasty. That was not Johnny Ray's nature, but his remarks stung and made her wonder if she was being blamed for all the hard feelings among the townspeople.

Later that day in the cloakroom Ruby saw Johnny Ray slipping a piece of cardboard inside one of his shoes to cover the holes in the worn-out sole. She turned away quickly so that he would not know she had seen, but she couldn't get that picture out of her head for the longest time.

Some folks in town were no longer speaking. People who had been neighbors and/or best friends for years turned their backs on one another on the street. Some brothers and sisters, even parents and their children, were angry with each other.

After the next town meeting, which lasted only fifteen minutes before it blew up, Ruby and Miss Arbutus walked home in the cold dark night without a word, but each was thinking the same disturbing thought. When that evil wind blew into Way Down, exactly what did it bring? Previously they had felt sure it brought economic hardships. But now? Now they wondered if perhaps the evil wind had brought the treasure.

22

TEMPERATURES DROPPED SHARPLY, AND A FOOT OF SNOW fell in March for the first time in anyone's memory. The miners' children didn't go to school. Even when buses were able to navigate the mountain roads again, some kids couldn't make it because they had no boots or clothing that was adequate against the weather.

People were coming down with cold-related illnesses, and Mr. Doctor was working such long, hard hours that he had to bring in assistants. The children of Way Down no longer played games in the streets. Even without the cold weather, they were too sad to enjoy themselves.

The Shimpock children no longer carried the familiar brown paper bags. There was nothing to put in them. Ruby tried to share her lunch with Becky, but she refused Ruby's charity, opting instead to huddle with others from Shimpock at lunch break, hungry and cold.

* * *

Though March had come in like a lion, it went out like a lamb, as the old saying goes, and the mayor took heart again. Maybe the people would be nicer to each other in warm weather. He sent out a plea through *The Way Down Deep Daily* for citizens to put aside their grievances. He urged them to try to be reasonable so that they could hold a meeting with cool heads prevailing.

In the meantime Archibald Ward's gold doubloons and pieces of eight had been sold for millions, and the money currently sat in a fancy New York bank, collecting huge sums of interest but remaining useless to the residents of Way Down. Folks sarcastically remarked that the treasure might as well have stayed in the ground.

On Monday night, April 18, the mayor tried again. It was Judge Elbert Deel's week to hold court, and because of his many years of experience in settling all kinds of disputes, he was asked by Mayor Chambers if he would preside over this meeting. He thought possibly the good folks would behave more appropriately for an honorable judge. The judge agreed to give it a try.

Again all the children, including Ruby, sat together on benches along the back wall of the courtroom. This meeting started off respectfully, as they all had done in the past, but as soon as the suggestions began to roll in, the tension built and tempers flared. Once again the participants ceased listening to their neighbors, raised their voices, shook fingers in each other's faces, and in general behaved exactly like politicians fighting over the budget.

The more Judge Deel banged his gavel, the louder the people quarreled. Not having any effect with the gavel, the judge finally tossed it aside. At this point the children were beginning to look toward the door, ready to bolt. But before they could do so, Judge Deel stood up and said in a commanding voice, "Suffer little children, and forbid them not, to come unto me: for of such is the kingdom of heaven!"

Upon hearing a verse from the Bible, some people immediately shut up. Others continued ranting. The children felt compelled to stay.

The judge repeated the verse. "Suffer little children, and forbid them not, to come unto me: for of such is the kingdom of heaven!"

At that, almost everybody sat down and listened. There was mumbling and grumbling in low tones, but most people now focused their eyes and ears on the judge. Then everybody together turned to look at the children where they sat lined up on their benches along the back wall of the courtroom. The realization came over the adults that these children were the only ones in town who had not yelled and screamed at each other during the past weeks. They had been quiet observers, perhaps a little bewildered and embarrassed by the actions of their parents, but they had been more grown-up than the grown-ups.

"And a little child shall lead them," Judge Deel said softly.

Silence lay thick over the room for the first time in all the meetings.

"Ruby found this treasure," Judge Deel said. "She did not have to share it. She could have kept it all for herself. But she gave it to the town. I move that Ruby will be the one who decides how it should be spent."

Immediately a voice called out, "I second that motion."

The judge gestured for the mayor to take over the meeting.

"All in favor?" the mayor asked hopefully, tentatively.

The room erupted in ayes. Then there was applause for Ruby.

"Ruby, will you accept this responsibility?" Mayor Chambers asked her.

Ruby leapt to her feet and cried in a tearful voice, "No, please. I don't want everybody hollering at me!"

A soft ripple of embarrassed laughter moved through the room. Then the grown-ups could not look at one another, but instead gazed at the floor and changed positions in their chairs. How had they let things deteriorate to this sorry state where the kids were ashamed of them?

"We will make a pledge to abide by your decision," the mayor said to Ruby, and the room burst into ayes again.

"But I'm only thirteen years old. Am I smart enough?" Ruby said almost in a whisper.

"You, of all people here, Ruby, are a product of Way Down," the judge spoke up again. "This town has raised you. Please do this for them."

Ruby looked at the faces of the townspeople. Every eye in the room was on her. And she saw no dirty looks among them.

Reluctantly she agreed. "I'll do my best."

* * *

As Ruby walked home with Miss Arbutus that night, she asked her advice. "Please tell me what to do."

"No," Miss Arbutus said bluntly. "This is something you have to do by yourself, Ruby. Nobody can help you."

It was next to the last Friday in April, and warmth was returning to the earth. All the kids were back in school, but they had had a hard winter and were not their usual lively selves. In fact, they were so quiet that Miss Duke was troubled. With her own life now filled with happiness, it was hard to see her young pupils hurting.

"Johnny Ray Springstep!" she interrupted her class that morning during a parts-of-speech exercise.

Johnny Ray sprang to his feet. Miss Duke had not bugged him for a long time, and he was startled. "Yes, ma'am?"

"Talk!" she commanded.

"Beg your pardon, ma'am?" Johnny Ray said.

"Talk, Johnny Ray. Talk out loud. Tell a silly story. Please. Something!"

The kids eyed her suspiciously. Was she going to act crazy again?

"It's just that *y'all* are way too quiet," she said, emphasizing the word *y'all*. She looked at Becky Trueheart, whose cinnamon eyes crinkled as her face lit up with a smile.

"Yeah, Johnny Ray," Becky said. "Talk!"

Then others took up the chant. "Talk, Johnny Ray, talk!"

And Johnny Ray understood. He smiled, too, and blushed.

"Miss Duke, I can't think of anything to say right now, but I'm sure it's just a temporary condition."

After that the kids began to feel close to one another again, and now to their teacher as well. In fact, they looked forward to Miss Duke's class more than any other.

And Ruby's spirits were raised. Yes! Things would surely work out.

Exactly one week later at twilight Ruby was taking Tripod for a short walk on the Way Up That-a-Way trail when she was startled by the sight of a big bald man standing on the side of the hill ahead of her. He seemed as tall as the trees. He twinkled blue all over and he was wearing cowboy boots, just as Rita had said.

"Look, Tripod!" she said excitedly. "It's Baldy!"

Immediately Tripod began to bark; then he bolted up the path with Ruby close behind him. After a winter with little exercise, however, Ruby found that running up a hillside winded her, and she had to stop to catch her breath. Now looking up to where she had seen Baldy, she found the spot empty. He had disappeared, and so had Tripod.

"Tripod!" Ruby called. "Tripod! Come back!"

But there was no movement on the mountainside, and no sound except for a few late birds calling good night to one another.

"Tripod!" she called again, but before the word was out of her mouth there was Baldy standing on the path right in front of her, larger than life. Tripod came out of the shadows and ran up to him, wagging his tail like crazy.

"Didn't I tell you the people in this time would be good to you?" Baldy said to the dog as he stooped and patted him on the head.

"Thank you for saving him from the trap," Ruby said to Baldy.

"Sure thing. It's part of my job."

"Oh? What is your job?"

"Night watchman."

"You're a night watchman?"

"Yeah. Each night, between twilight and dawn, I travel through time checking on my town," Baldy said. "I skip around from year to year, but I manage to cover most of the two centuries, from 1755 all the way up to now, 1955. You know—making sure everything is going as it should."

"And that's how you found Tripod caught in the trap?"

"Yeah. I think it was in 1837 or thereabouts. So I brought him here to your time, where he could get better medical care and have a chance to live."

"Tripod came from 1837?"

"Yep! And how did you like that pumpkin I left on your porch?"

"You did that, too?"

"It came from the year 1872. The Wards had huge pumpkins that year."

"And lifted the chest out of the hole for me?"

"Sure did."

"Then thanks again."

"That part was easy for me. You had already done the hard work."

"Do you know what happened to my goat?"

"Sure I know. He died."

"I mean, what happened to his body? It wasn't in the basket."

"I took it somewhere else 'cause I knew you'd be digging in that spot. That's why you didn't see his shadow again. But don't worry. He's a happy goat where he is."

"Who are you?"

"I told you. I'm the night watchman."

"But what's your name?"

He laughed. "Don't you know?"

Ruby shook her head slowly.

"Yes, you do, Ruby. You know me," he said. "Just as I know you."

"Are you Archibald Ward?" Ruby asked hopefully. "The founder of Way Down?"

Baldy laughed again and did not answer.

"I have to make a decision," she said to him. "I have to tell the town how to spend the money. What shall I tell them?"

"You don't have to ask me, Ruby. You know already. It's been in your heart all along. That's why you were the one to find the treasure."

Baldy laughed long and loud, and then he evaporated into the gathering darkness, but Ruby could hear the echo of his laughter and see a blue mist floating among the treetops. Thoughtfully, she walked home with Tripod.

She slept soundly that night, and when she woke up at the crack of dawn, her decision was made. Of course. It was the *only* answer. And Baldy was right. It had been in her heart all the time. She smiled at the rising sun and was warmed.

23

AFTER BREAKFAST RUBY CALLED MISS ARBUTUS ASIDE AND told her the decision she had made. She watched tears well up into Miss Arbutus's eyes.

"So you like it?" Ruby asked.

Miss Arbutus hugged her. "I love it, and I am very, very proud of you. I knew you would know exactly what to do."

"Will you help me write it all down on paper with the proper words, before I present it to the town?"

"I will, but I think we should ask a teacher and a writer to assist us."

"You mean Miss Duke and Mr. Crawford?"

"Yes."

That very afternoon Ruby and Tripod, Miss Arbutus, Miss Duke, and Mr. Crawford barricaded themselves in the dining room and wrote out Ruby's proclamation for the distribution of the treasure of Way Down Deep. When they were finished, Miss Arbutus called the mayor and suggested he announce another meeting of the townspeople that night. Ruby had made her decision. Of course, everybody on The Roost party line was listening in, so the news spread rapidly.

It was the last day of April, and the entire population of Way Down, plus those who lived in the new houses on Highway 99, poured into the courtroom with the same air of excited expectation they had carried with them to the very first meeting. They greeted one another with kind regards, handshakes, and hugs, as in the days before their greed had come between them. When Mayor Chambers called the meeting to order, there was not another sound in the room. First, he reminded the good folks of the pledge they had made to abide by Ruby's decision, and to keep negative comments, if they had any, to themselves. Then he turned to Ruby, who was once again sitting in the front row with Miss Arbutus. Miss Duke and Mr. Crawford sat on the other side of her.

"The floor is yours, young lady," the mayor said to her.

Ruby stood up and walked to the front of the room. When she looked at her audience, she saw all different colors of eyes watching her. The faces were serious and expectant. And she was suddenly afraid. Suppose they were disppointed in her decision? She swallowed hard. She would just spit it out, she thought, and sit down quickly.

She cleared her throat nervously and spoke as loudly and clearly as she could manage. "All the money from the treasure will go to the children of the Way Down Deep School."

No one stirred for a moment. Then one person clapped. Another person did the same. Everyone applauded very politely, but they did not seem overjoyed.

"Let me explain," Ruby went on. And she read the speech that Miss Duke, Mr. Crawford, and Miss Arbutus had helped her prepare. "This means that the riches will go first of all to hire more staff and qualified teachers to develop accelerated math and science programs with real science labs, also several creative arts departments. A summer program will be established, the playground and sports field expanded, more classrooms built, also a library, a gymnasium, an auditorium, a swimming pool, and a cafeteria that will serve two free meals a day so that no child will ever go hungry."

When she paused for breath, the room exploded with applause. Ruby felt her face finally relax into a smile. Yes! They liked it! But she was not finished.

She held up one hand. "Second, generous donations will add to the public library collection and keep it funded. Third, and most important, all students graduating from Way Down School will be sent to an institution of higher learning of their choice to pursue their dreams. In return, the graduates will promise to turn a small percentage of their future earnings back into the treasury for the perpetuation of the legacy."

Now the people really were overjoyed, all their petty fights forgotten. They applauded, cheered, hugged one another, and came forward to hug Ruby.

Mr. Dales, the banker, who knew all about money, asked to be recognized.

"Yes, speak," the mayor said.

"Kids really are the best possible investment we could make

in our community and its future. With interest and new reve-
nues from the graduates, the treasure will go on indefinitely."

"One more thing!" Ruby had to yell to be heard above the
uproar.

The people shushed one another and listened.

"There is a surprise that the mayor will announce tomorrow," Ruby said. Then, with a great deal of happiness in her
heart, she sat down beside Miss Arbutus.

Mr. Crawford, accompanied by Miss Duke with a brand-
new engagement ring on her finger, rushed out immediately to
write up yet another chapter for his book, but not before Miss
Duke gave Ruby a hug.

Mr. Bear, the principal, overwhelmed with the good news,
sat down beside Lucy Elkins and actually burst into tears.

"I can't believe all the prayers I have offered up for my cubs
are being answered," he said when he was able to speak again.
"And that I am actually going to have a secretary to boot!"

"Every principal should have a secretary," Lucy said.

"And do you have anybody in mind?" Mr. Bear said eagerly.
"I could use somebody right away."

"Yes, I do have somebody in mind," Lucy said. "I taught
myself to type when I was young. I am very good with num-
bers. I would make an excellent receptionist. I have a pleasant
telephone voice. And I love helping people, especially children."

"Can you report Monday morning?" Mr. Bear said.

"Indeed I can," Lucy said as her heart began to sing. At last she would be able to pay her own way in the world, which is a wonderful thing.

The next day Mr. Bear and the mayor sent all the school buses, plus extra public buses, to go pick up the miners' children and Shimpock children and their parents to come to town to tell them the good news and to celebrate with them. It was a beautiful May Day with a gentle breeze. The brown mountains of winter had gone to green again, and flowers were blooming everywhere.

The people gathered in the school yard, where tables were overflowing with good food and drink. The announcement was made public early on, but of course the word had leaked already, and nobody was caught by surprise.

"And now I wish to give you another bit of good news," the mayor said to the crowd. "Ruby wants to make sure we don't forget the miners and others who are out of work right now. She wants us to use some of this money for emergency relief."

There were mumbles and nods of approval.

"It has been decided that a special temporary fund will be set aside for food, clothing, and other necessities while the unemployment problem persists."

At this announcement the cheers and applause once again filled the little valley that lay way down deep between the mountains.

Some of the teachers had set up a maypole, and as the barefoot children twined their ribbons around it and sang together, they could see their bright futures like shining cities over the mountaintops.

Johnny Ray Springstep was reminded of the morning he had felt fireworks going off in his head when he was first introduced to chemistry.

Connie Lynn and Bonnie Clare Fuller saw themselves as missionaries in Africa, while their sister, Sunny Gaye, dreamed of becoming a church music director.

Becky Trueheart saw her true path in life as that of becoming a teacher as fine as Miss Duke.

Peter Reeder understood that he really *could* become a veterinarian.

Slim Morgan envisioned his photographs in *National Geographic*.

Ruby, with her three-legged dog prancing at her heels, thought she had all the time in the world to make up her mind. She could be anything she wanted to be, but whatever she chose to do with her life, she would do it here in Way Down Deep.